D0946410

Aunt Crete's Emancipation

GRACE LIVINGSTON HILL

Aunt Crete's Emancipation

Fleming H. Revell Company
Old Tappan, New Jersey

Library of Congress Cataloging in Publication Data

Hill, Grace Livingston, 1865–1947.
    Aunt Crete's emancipation.

    (Classic series ; 7)
    I. Title.   II. Series: Hill, Grace Livingston,
1865–1947.   Classic series ; 7.
PS3515.I486A94   1984   813'.52   83-11081
ISBN 0-8007-1363-X

Contents

Introduction

Behind the romantic fairy-tale atmosphere of many of my mother's books was her persistent conviction that happy endings are to be expected for those who are truly in the family of God. Through her own intimate acquaintance and her experiences watching people's tangled lives in her father's pastorates, she was utterly convinced that for a true child of God it is always "better farther on," no matter what fiery furnace may be in the present earthly path.

Perhaps this delightful confidence in final justice has played a large part in attracting her host of readers. She never thought of her strong faith as being "pie in the sky bye and bye" but as a solid rock foundation to rest upon here and now. Many a time I have watched her lay down her burdens—and she had plenty of them—and take her stand on those sure promises. She could write of happy endings because she had experienced them.

Not every one of her books spells out the way of salvation in so many words. This was partly because some publishers shied from "religion" as such, and partly because she never forced her faith in her Saviour on people who did not want to be saved. But all her writings were based on the promises she had proved to be true for herself.

Much as she loved beautiful things, to her the most beautiful were the changed lives of those born into the family of God.

RUTH LIVINGSTON HILL

Aunt Crete's Emancipation

Chapter 1

A Telegram and a Flight

W ho's at the front door?" asked Luella's mother, coming in from the kitchen with a dish towel in her hand. "I thought I heard the doorbell."

"Luella's gone to the door," said her sister from her vantage point at the crack of the sitting room door. "It looks to me like a telegraph boy."

"It couldn't be, Crete," said Luella's mother impatiently, coming to see for herself. "Who would telegraph now that Hannah's dead?"

Lucretia was short and dumpy, with the comfortable, patient look of the maiden aunt that knows she is indispensable because she will meekly take all the burdens that no one else wants to bear. Her sister could easily look over her head into the hall, and her gaze was penetrative and alert.

"I'm sure I don't know, Carrie," said Lucretia apprehensively, "but I'm all of a tremble. Telegrams are dreadful things."

"Nonsense, Crete, you always act like such a baby. Hurry up, Luella. Don't stop to read it. Your aunt Crete will have a fit. Wasn't there anything to pay? Who is it for?"

Luella, a rather stout young woman in stylish attire, with her mother's keen features unsoftened by sentiment, advanced, irreverently tearing open her mother's telegram and

13

reading it as she came. It was one of the family grievances that Luella was stout like her aunt instead of tall and slender like her mother. The aunt always felt secretly that they somehow blamed her for being of that type. "It makes one so hard to fit," Luella's mother remarked frequently, and adding with a disparaging glance at her sister's dumpy form, "So impossible!"

At such times the aunt always wrinkled up her pleasant little forehead into a V upside down, and trotted off to her kitchen, or her buttonholes, or whatever was the present task, sighing helplessly. She tried to be the best that she could always; but one couldn't help one's figure, especially when one was partly dependent on one's family for support, and dressmakers and tailors took so much money. It was bad enough to have one stout figure to fit in the family without two; and the aunt always felt called upon to have as little dressmaking done as possible, in order that Luella's figure might be improved from the slender treasury. "Clothes do make a big difference," she reflected. And sometimes when she was all alone in the twilight, and there was really nothing that her alert conscience could possibly put her hand to doing for the moment, she amused herself by thinking what kind of dress she would buy, and who should make it, if she should suddenly attain a fortune. But this was a harmless amusement, inasmuch as she never let it make her discontented with her lot, or ruffle her placid brow for an instant.

But just now she was "all of a tremble," and the V in her forehead was rapidly becoming a double V. She watched Luella's dismayed face with growing alarm.

"For goodness' sake alive!" said Luella, flinging herself

into the most comfortable rocker, and throwing her mother's telegram on the table. "That's not to be tolerated! Something 'll have to be done. We'll have to go to the shore at once, Mother. I should die of mortification to have a country cousin come around just now. What would the Grandons think if they saw him? I can't afford to ruin all my chances for a cousin I've never seen. Mother, you simply must do something. I won't stand it!"

"What in the world are you talking about, Luella?" said her mother impatiently. "Why didn't you read the telegram aloud, or why didn't you give it to me at once? Where are my glasses?"

The aunt waited meekly while her sister found her glasses, and read the telegram.

"Well, I declare! That is provoking to have him turn up just now of all times. Something must be done, of course. We can't have a gawky westerner around in the way. And, as you say, we've never seen him. It can't make much difference to him whether he sees us or not. We can hurry off, and be conveniently out of the way. It's probably only a duty visit he's paying, anyway. Hannah's been dead ten years, and I always heard the child was more like his father than his mother. Besides, Hannah married and went away to live when I was only a little girl. I really don't think Donald has much claim on us. What a long telegram! It must have cost a lot. Was it paid for? It shows he knows nothing of the world, or he would have put it in a few words. Well, we'll have to get away at once."

She crumpled the telegram into a ball, and flung it to the table again; but it fell wide of its mark, and dropped to the floor instead. The aunt patiently stooped and picked it up, smoothing out the crushed yellow paper.

"Hannah's boy!" she said gently, and she touched the yellow paper as if it had been something sacred.

> Am taking a trip east, and shall make you a little visit if convenient. Will be with you sometime on Thursday.
> DONALD GRANT

She sat down suddenly in the nearest chair. Somehow the relief from anxiety had made her knees weak. "Hannah's boy!" she murmured again, and laid her hand caressingly over the telegram, smoothing down a torn place in the edge of the paper.

Luella and her mother were discussing plans. They had decided that they must leave on the early train the next morning, before there was any chance of the western visitor's arriving.

"Goodness! Look at Aunt Crete," said Luella, laughing. "She looks as if she had seen a ghost. Her lips are all white."

"Crete, you oughtn't to be such a fool. As if a telegram would hurt you! There's nobody left to be worried about like that. Why don't you use your reason a little?"

"Hannah's boy is really coming!" beamed Aunt Crete, ignoring their scorn of herself.

"Upon my word! Aunt Crete, you look as if it were something to be glad about, instead of a downright calamity."

"Glad, of course I'm glad, Luella. Wouldn't you be glad to see your oldest sister's child? Hannah was always very dear to me. I can see her now the way she looked when she went away, so tall and slim and pretty——"

"Not if she'd been dead for a century or so, and I'd never

seen the child, and he was a gawky, embarrassing creature who would spoil the prospects of the people I was supposed to love," retorted Luella. "Aunt Crete, don't you care the least bit for my happiness? Do you want it all spoiled?"

"Why, of course not, dearie," beamed Aunt Crete, "but I don't see how it will spoil your happiness. I should think you'd want to see him yourself."

"Aunt Crete! The idea! He's nothing to me. You know he's lived away out in the wild west all his life. He probably never had much schooling, and doesn't know how to dress or behave in polite society. I heard he went away off up in the Klondike somewhere, and worked in a mine. You can imagine just what a wild, ignorant creature he will be. If Clarence Grandon should see him, he might imagine my family were all like that, and then where would I be?"

"Yes, Crete, I'm surprised at you. You've been so anxious all along for Luella to shine in society, and now you talk just as if you didn't care in the least what happened," put in Luella's mother.

"But what can you do?" asked Aunt Crete. "You can't tell him not to come—your own sister's child!"

"Oh, how silly you are, Crete!" said her sister. "No, of course we can't very well tell him not to come, as he hasn't given us a chance; for this telegram is evidently sent on the way. It is dated Chicago, and he hasn't given us a trace of an address. He doesn't live in Chicago. He's very likely almost here, and may arrive any time tomorrow. Now you know we've simply got to go to the shore next week, for the rooms are all engaged at the hotel, and paid for, and we might as well hurry up and get off tonight or early in the morning, and escape him. Luella would die of mortification if she had to visit with that fellow and give up her trip to the shore. As you weren't going anyway, you can receive him. It will keep him quietly at home, for he won't expect an old woman to go out with him, and show him the sights, so nobody will notice him much, and there won't be a lot of talk. If he looks very ridiculous, and that prying Mrs. Brown next door speaks of it, you might explain he's the son of an old school friend who went out west to live years ago——"

"Oh Carrie!" exclaimed Aunt Crete, "that wouldn't be true; and, besides, he can't be so very bad as that. And even if he is, I shall love him—for he's Hannah's boy."

"Love him all you want to," sniffed her sister, "but for pity's sake don't let the neighbors know what relation he is."

"That's just like you, Aunt Crete," said Luella in a hurt tone. "You've known me and pretended to love me all your life. I'm almost like your own child, and yet you take up with this unknown nephew, and say you'll love him in spite of all the trouble he's making me."

Aunt Crete doubled the V in her forehead, and wiped away the beads of perspiration. Somehow it always seemed that she was in the wrong. Would she be understood in heaven? she wondered.

Luella and her mother went on planning. They advised what Aunt Crete was to do after they left.

"There's the raspberries and blackberries not done up yet, Crete, but I guess you can manage alone. You always do the biggest part of the canning, anyway. I'm awfully sorry about your sewing, Crete. I meant to fit your two thin dresses before we went away, but the dressmaker made Luella's things so much more elaborate than I expected that we really haven't had a minute's time, what with all the lace insertion she left for us to sew on. Perhaps you better run down to Miss Mason, and see if she has time to fit them, if you think you can't wait till we get back. You'll hardly be going out much while we're gone, you know."

"Oh, I'll be all right," said Aunt Crete happily. "I guess I can fix up my gray lawn for while Donald's here."

"Donald! Nonsense! It won't matter what you wear while he's here. He'll never know a calico from a silk. Now look here, Crete, you've got to be awfully careful, or you'll let out when we went off. There's no use in his finding out we didn't want to see him. You wouldn't want to hurt his feelings, you know. Your own sister's child!"

"No, of course not," agreed Aunt Crete, though there was a troubled look in her eyes. She never liked prevarication; and, when she was left with some polite fabrication to excuse her relatives out of something they wanted to shirk, she nearly always got it twisted so that it was either an out-and-out lie, which horrified her, or else let the whole thing "out of the bag," as Luella said.

But there was little time for discussion; for Luella and her mother had a great deal of packing to do, and Aunt Crete had the dinner to get and the house to set in order, surreptitiously, for the expected guest.

They hurried away the next morning in a whirl of bags and suitcases and parasols and umbrellas. They had baggage enough for a year in Europe, although they expected to stay only two or three weeks at the shore at most. Aunt Crete helped them into the station cab, ran back to the house for Luella's new raincoat, back again for the veil and her sister's gloves, and still a third time to bring the new book, which had been set aside for reading on the journey.

Then at last they were gone, and with one brief sigh of satis-faction Aunt Crete permitted herself to reflect that she was actually left alone to receive a dear guest all her own.

Never in all her maiden existence had she had this plea-sure before. She might use the best china, and have three kinds of pie at once, yes, and plum cake if she chose. Boys like pie and cake. Donald would be a big, nice boy.

What did it matter to her if he was awkward and from the west? He was in a large sense her own. Hannah was gone, and there was no one else to take a closer place. Who but his mother's sister should have the right to mother him for a while? He would be her own as Luella never had been, be-cause there was always Luella's mother to take the first place. Besides, Luella had been a disappointing baby. Even in her infancy she had developed an independence that scorned kissing and cuddling. Luella always had too many selfish interests on hand to have time for breathing out love and baby graces to admiring subjects. Her frown was always quicker than her smile. But somehow Aunt Crete felt that it would be different with this boy, and her heart swelled within her as she hurried into the house to make ready for his coming.

The front hall was littered with rose leaves. Luella had shaken a bunch of roses to get rid of the loose leaves, and had found they were all loose leaves; therefore she flung them down upon the floor. She had meant to wear them with her new pongee traveling suit. It looked well to wear roses on a journey, for it suggested a possible admirer. But the roses had not held out, and now Aunt Crete must sweep them up.

A glance into the parlor showed peanut shells scattered

over the floor and on the table. A few of Luella's friends had come in for a few minutes the evening before, and they had indulged in peanuts, finishing up by throwing the shells at one another amid shouts of hilarious laughter. Aunt Crete went for the broom and dustpan. If he came early, the hall and parlor must be in order first.

Luella and her mother had little time to waste, for the tickets were barely bought and the trunks checked before the train thundered up. It was a through vestibuled train; and, as Luella struggled up the steps of one car with her heavy suitcase, a tall young man with dark, handsome eyes and a distinguished manner swung himself down the steps of the next car.

"Hello, Luella!" called a voice from a pony cart by the platform. "You're not going away today, are you? Thought you said you weren't going till next week."

"Circumstances made it necessary," called Luella from the top step of the car while the porter held up the suitcase for her to take. "I'm running away from a backwoods cousin that's coming to visit. I'll write and tell you all about it. Good-bye. Sorry I can't be at your house tomorrow night, but it couldn't be helped."

Then Luella turned another gaze upon the handsome stranger, who was standing on the platform just below her, looking about interestedly. She thought he had looked at her more than casually; and, as she settled herself in the seat, she glanced down at her pongee traveling suit consciously, feeling that he could but have thought she looked well.

He was still standing on the platform as the train moved out, and Luella could see the girl in the pony cart turn her attention to him. She half wished she were sitting in the pony cart too. It would be interesting to find out who he was. Luella preened herself, and settled her large hat in front of the strip of mirror between the windows, and then looked around the car that she might see who were her fellow passengers.

"Well, I'm glad we're off," said her mother nervously. "I was afraid as could be your cousin might come in on that early through train before we got started. It would have been trying if he'd come just as we were getting away. I don't know how we could have explained it."

"Yes," said Luella. "I'm glad we're safely off. He'll never suspect now."

It was just at that moment that the grocery boy arrived at the back door with a crate of red raspberries.

"Land alive!" said Miss Crete disappointedly. "I hoped those wouldn't come till tomorrow." She bustled about, taking the boxes out of the crate so that the boy might take it back; and before she was done the doorbell rang.

"Land alive!" said Miss Crete again as she wiped her hands on the kitchen towel and hurried to the front door, taking off her apron as she went. "I do hope he hasn't come yet. I haven't cleared off that breakfast table; and, if he should happen to come out, there's three plates standing."

But the thought had come too late. The dining room door was stretched wide open, and the table in full view. The front door was guarded only by the wire screen. The visitor had been able to take full notes, if he so desired.

Chapter 2

The Backwoods Cousin

Miss Lucretia opened the screen, and noticed the fine appearance of the young man standing there. He was not shabby enough for an agent. Someone had made a mistake, she supposed. She waited pleasantly for him to tell his errand.

"Is this where Mrs. Carrie Burton lives?" he asked, removing his hat courteously.

And, when she answered, "Yes," his whole face broke into dancing eagerness.

"Is this my Aunt Carrie? I wonder"; and he held out a tentative, appealing hand for welcome. "I'm Donald Grant."

"Oh!" said Miss Lucretia delightedly, "Oh!" and she took his hand in both her own. "No, I ain't your Aunt Carrie, I'm your Aunt Crete; but I'm just as glad to see you. I didn't think you'd be so big and handsome. Your Aunt Carrie isn't home. They've just—why—that is—they are—they had planned to be at the shore for three weeks, and they'll be real sorry when they know——" This last sentence was added with extra zeal, for Aunt Crete exulted in the fact that Carrie and Luella would indeed be sorry if they could look into their home for one instant and see the guest from whom they had run away. She felt sure that if they had known how

25

fine-looking a young man he was, they would have stayed and been proud of him.

"I'm sorry they are away," said the young man, stooping to kiss Aunt Crete's plump, comfortable cheek, "but I'm mighty glad you're at home, Aunt Crete," he said with genuine pleasure. "I'm going to like you for all I'm worth to make up for the absence of my aunt and cousin. You say they have gone to the shore. When will they be at home? Is their stay there almost up?"

"Why, no," said Aunt Crete, flushing uncomfortably. "They haven't been gone long. And they've engaged their rooms there for three weeks at a big hotel. Luella, she's always been bound to go to one of those big places where rich people go, the Traymore. It's advertised in all the papers. I expect you've seen it sometimes. It's one of the most expensive places at the shore. I've almost a notion to write and tell them to come home, for I'm sure they'll be sorry when they hear about you, but you see it's this way. There's a young man been paying Luella some attention, and he's going down there soon; I don't know but he's there already, and his mother and sister are spending the whole season there, so Luella had her heart set on going down and boarding at the same hotel."

"Ah, I see," said the nephew. "Well, it wouldn't do to spoil my cousin's good time. Perhaps we can run down to the shore for a few days ourselves after we get acquainted. Say, Aunt Crete, am I too late for a bite of breakfast? I was so tired of the stuff they had on the dining car I thought I'd save up my appetite till I got here, for I was sure you'd have a bite of bread and butter, anyway."

"Bless your dear heart, yes," said Aunt Crete, delighted to have the subject turned; for she had a terrible fear she would yet tell a lie about the departure of her sister and niece, and a lie was a calamity not always easily avoided in a position like hers. "You just sit down here, you dear boy, and wait about two minutes till I set the coffeepot over the fire and cut some more bread. It isn't a mite of trouble, for I hadn't cleared off the breakfast table yet. In fact, I hadn't rightly finished my own breakfast, I was so busy getting to rights. The grocery boy came, and—well, I never can eat much when folks are going—I mean when I'm alone," she finished triumphantly.

She hurried out into the dining room to get the table cleared off, but Donald followed her. She tried to scuttle the plates together and remove all traces of the number of guests at the meal just past, but she could not be sure whether he noticed the table or not.

"May I help you?" asked the young man, grabbing Luella's plate and cup, and following her into the kitchen. "It's so good to get into a real home again with somebody who belongs to me. You know Father is in Mexico, and I've been in the university for the last four years."

"The university!" Aunt Crete's eyes shone. "Do you have universities out west? My! Won't Luella be astonished? I guess she thinks out west is all woods."

Donald's eyes danced.

"We have a few good schools out there," he said quietly.

While they were eating the breakfast that Aunt Crete prepared in an incredibly short space of time, Donald asked a great many questions. What did his aunt and cousin look like? Was Aunt Carrie like her, or like his mother? And Luella, had she been to college? And what did she look like?

Aunt Crete told him mournfully that Luella was more like herself than like her mother. "And it seems sometimes as if she blamed me for it," said the patient aunt. "It makes it hard, her being a sort of society girl, and wanting to look so fine. Dumpy figures like mine don't dress up pretty, you know. No, Luella never went to college. She didn't take much to books. She liked having a good time with young folks better. She's been wanting to go down to the shore and be at a real big hotel for three summers now, but Carrie never felt able to afford it before. We've been saving up all winter for Luella to have this treat, and I do hope she'll have a good time. It's real hard on her, having to stay right home all the time when all her girl friends go off to the shore. But you see she's got in with some real wealthy people who stay at expensive places, and she isn't satisfied to go to a common boardinghouse. It must be nice to have money and go to a big hotel. I've never been in one myself, but Luella has, and she's told all about it. I should think it would be grand to live that way awhile with not a thing to do."

"They ought to have taken you along, Aunt Crete," said the young man. "I do hope I didn't keep you at home to entertain me."

"Oh, no, bless your heart," said the aunt, "I wasn't going. I never go anywhere. Why, what kind of a figure would I cut there? It would spoil all Luella's good time to have me around, I'm so short-waisted. She always wants me to wear a coat when I go anywhere with her, so people won't see how short-waisted I am."

"Nonsense," said Donald. "I think you are lovely, Aunt

Crete. You've got such pretty white hair, all wavy like Mother's; and you've got a fine face. Luella ought to be proud to have you."

Aunt Crete blushed over the compliment, and choking tears of joy throbbed for a minute in her throat.

"Now hear the boy!" she exclaimed. "Donald, do have another cup of coffee."

After breakfast Aunt Crete showed her guest to his room, and then hurried down to get the stack of dishes out of the way before he came down again. But he appeared in the kitchen door in a few minutes.

"Give me a dish and some berries," he demanded. "I'm going to help you."

And despite all her protests he helped with such vigor that by twelve o'clock twenty-one jars of crimson berries stood in a shining row on the kitchen table, and Aunt Crete was dishing up a savory dinner for two, with her face shining as brightly as if she had done nothing but play the whole morning.

"We did well, didn't we?" said Donald as he ate his dinner. "I haven't had such a good time since I went camping in the Klondike. Now after we get these dishes washed you are going to take a nice long nap. You look tired and warm."

Aunt Crete protested that she was not tired, but Donald insisted. "I want you to get nice and rested up, because tomorrow we're going shopping. By the way, I've brought you a present." He sprang up from the table, and went to his suitcase to get it.

Aunt Crete's heart beat with anticipation as he handed her a little white box. What if it should be a breastpin? How she would like that! She had worn her mother's, a braid of hair under a glass, with a gold band under it, ever since she was grown up, and sometimes she felt as if it was a little old-fashioned. Luella openly scoffed at it, and laughed at her for wearing it, but no one ever suggested getting her a new one, and, if she had ventured to buy one for herself, she knew they would have thought her extravagant.

She opened the box with excited fingers, and there inside was a little leather case. Donald touched a spring, and it flew open and disclosed a lovely star made all of seed pearls, reposing on white velvet. It was a breastpin indeed, and one fit for a queen. Fortunately Aunt Crete did not know enough about jewelry to realize what it cost, or her breath might have been taken away. As it was, she was stunned for the moment. Such a beautiful pin, and for her! She could scarcely believe it. She gazed and gazed, and then, laying the box on the table, rose up and took Donald's face in her two toil-worn hands, and kissed him.

"I'm glad you like it," he said with a pleased smile. "I wasn't quite sure what to get, but the salesman told me these were always nice. Now let's get at these dishes."

In a daze of happiness Aunt Crete washed the dishes while Donald wiped them, and then despite her protest he made her go upstairs and lie down.

When had she ever taken a nap in the daytime before? Not since she was a little girl and fell from the second-story window. The family had rushed around her frightened, and put her to bed in the daytime, and for one whole day she had been waited upon and cared for tenderly. Then she had been able to get up, and the hard, careless, toilsome world had rushed on again for her. But the memory of that blessed day of rest, touched by gentleness, had lingered forever a bright spot in her memory. She had always been the one that did the hard things in her family, even when she was quite young.

Aunt Crete lay cautiously down upon her neatly made bed after she had attired herself in her best gown, a rusty black and white silk made over from one Luella had grown tired of, and clasped her hands blissfully on her breast, resting with her eyes wide open and a light of joy upon her face. She hardly felt it right to relax entirely, lest Donald might call her, but finally the unaccustomed position in the middle of the day sent her off into a real doze, and just about that time the telephone bell rang.

The telephone was in the sitting room downstairs. It had been put in at the time when the telephone company was putting them in free to introduce them in that suburb. It was ordinarily a source of great interest to the whole family, though it seldom rang except for Luella. Luella and her mother were exceedingly proud of its possession.

Donald was in the sitting room reading. He looked up from his paper, hesitated a moment, and then took down the receiver. Perhaps his aunt was asleep already, and he could attend to this without waking her.

"Hello; is this 53 M?"

Donald glanced at the number on the telephone, and answered, "Yes."

"Here you are, Atlantic. Here is Midvale," went on the voice of the operator at central.

"Hello! Is that you, Aunt Crete? This is Luella," came another girl's strident voice in hasty impatience. "What in the world were you so long about answering the phone for? I've been waiting here an age. Now, listen, Aunt Crete. For heaven's sake don't you tell that crazy cousin of ours where to find us, or like as not he'll take a notion to run down here and see us, and I should simply die of mortification if he did. This is a very swell hotel, and it would be fierce to have a backwoods relation appear on the scene. Now be sure you keep quiet. I'll never forgive you if you don't. And say, Aunt Crete, won't you please sew on the rest of that Val edging down the ruffles of the waist and on the skirt of my new lavender organdie, and do it up, and send it by mail? I forgot all about it. It's on the bed in the spare room, and the edging is started. You sew it on the way it is begun. You'll see. Now don't you go to sewing it on in the old way because it is quicker; for it doesn't look a bit pretty, and you've nothing much else to do, now we're gone, anyway. And say, Aunt Crete, would you mind going down to Peter's today, and telling Jennie I forgot all about getting those aprons to finish for the fair, and tell her you'll finish them for her? Do it today, because she has to send the box off by the end of the week. And Mother says you better clean the cellar right away, and she wondered if you'd feel equal to whitewashing it. I should think you'd like to do that, it's so cool this warm weather to be down cellar. And, Oh, yes, if you get lonesome and want something to do, I forgot to tell you I left those three flannel shirtwaists all cut out ready to be made in the upper bureau drawer of the spare room. Now don't read your eyes out the way you did the last time we went off and left you, and have to wear dark glasses for a week, because I have lots of things planned to do when I get home. I'm going to have Helena Bates for a week, and there'll be several lunches and picnics doing. Oh, say, Aunt Crete, Mother says, if there's any more pie cherries to be had, you better put up some, and be sure and stone them all. I just hate them with the seeds in. And I guess that's all, only don't forget you promised to have all those buttonholes worked for me in those underclothes I'm making, before I get back. Are you all right? Let me see. There was something else. Oh, yes, Mother says you don't need to get out the best china and make a great fuss as if you had grand company; he's only a country boy, you know. Say, Aunt Crete. Are you there? Why don't you answer? Aunt Crete! Hello! For pity's sake, what is the matter with this phone? Hello, central! Oh, dear! I suppose she's gone away. That's the way Aunt Crete always does!"

Donald, a strange, amused expression upon his face, stood listening and hesitating. He did not know exactly what to do. Without any intention at all he had listened to a conversation not intended for his ears. Should he answer and tell who he was? No, for that would but embarrass Luella. Neither would it do to call Aunt Crete now, for they would be sure to find out he had heard. Perhaps it was better to keep entirely still. There seemed to be nothing serious at stake. Ruffles and shirtwaists and gingham aprons for a guild and whitewashing the cellar! Nobody would die if none of them were done, and his blood boiled over the tone in which the invisible cousin at the other end of the wire had ordered Aunt Crete about. He could read the whole life story of the patient self-sacrifice on the one hand and imposition on the other. He felt strongly impelled to do something in the matter. A rebuke of some sort should be administered. How could it best be done?

Meantime Luella was fuming with the telephone girl, and the girl was declaring that she could get no answer from

Midvale anymore. Donald stood wickedly enjoying their discomfiture, and was at last rewarded by hearing Luella say: "Well, I guess I've said all I want to say, anyway; so you needn't ring them up again. I've got to go out boating now." The receiver at the shore clicked into place, and the connection was cut off.

Then the young man hung up the receiver at the Midvale end of the line, and sat down to think. Bit by bit he pieced together the story until he had very nearly made out the true state of affairs. So they were ashamed of him, and were trying to get away. Could it be possible that they had been the people that got on the train as he got off? Was that girl with the loud voice and the pongee suit his cousin? The voice over the telephone seemed like the one that had called to the girl in the pony cart. And had his eyes deceived him, or were there three plates on the breakfast table that morning? Poor Aunt Crete! He would give her the best time he knew how, and perhaps it was also set for him to give his cousin a lesson.

Chapter 3

A Wonderful Day

Aunt Crete woke up at last from an uncomfortable dream. She thought Carrie and Luella had come back, and were about to snatch Donald away from her and bear him off to the shore.

She arose in haste and smoothed her hair, astonished at the freshness of her own face in the glass. She was afraid she had overslept and lost some of the precious time with Donald. There was so much to ask him, and he was so good to look at. She hurried down and was received warmly. Donald's meditations had culminated in a plan.

"Sit down, Aunt Crete; are you sure you are rested? Then I want to talk. Suppose we run down to the shore and surprise the folks. How soon could you be ready?"

"Oh, dear heart! I couldn't do that!" exclaimed Aunt Crete, her face nevertheless alight with pleasure at the very thought.

"Why not? What's to hinder?"

"Oh, I never go. I always stay at home and attend to things."

"But that's no reason. Why couldn't things attend to themselves?"

"Why I couldn't leave the house alone."

"Now, what in the world could possibly happen to the

37

house that you could prevent by staying in it? Be reasonable, dear Aunt. You know the house won't run away while you are gone, and, if it does, I'll get you another one. You don't mean to tell me you never go off on a vacation. Then it's high time you went, and you'll have to stay longer to make up for lost time. Besides, I want your company. I've never seen the eastern coast, and expect to enjoy it hugely, but I need somebody to enjoy it with me. I can't half take things in alone. I want somebody my very own to go with me. That's what I came here for. I had thought of inviting you all to go down for a little trip, but, as the others are down there, why, we can join them."

Aunt Crete's face clouded. What would Luella say at having them appear on her horizon? The young man was all right, apparently, but there was no telling how angry Luella might be if her aunt came. She knew that Luella preferred to keep her in the background.

"I really couldn't go, dear," she said wistfully. "I'd like it with all my heart. And it would be specially nice to go with you, for I never had anybody to go round with me, not since your mother was a girl and used to take me with her wherever she went. I missed her dreadfully after she was married and went west. She was always so good to me."

The young man's face softened, and he reached his hand impulsively across the table, and grasped the toil-worn hand of his aunt.

"Well, you shall have somebody to go round with you now, Auntie; that is, if you'll let me. I'm not going to take 'No' for an answer. You just must go. We'll have a vacation all by ourselves, and do just as we please, and we'll bring up at the hotel where Aunt Carrie and Luella are, and surprise them."

"But, child, I can't!" said Aunt Crete in dismay, seeing his determination. "Why, I haven't any clothes suitable to wear away from home. We were all so busy getting Luella fixed out that there wasn't any time left for mine, and it didn't really matter about me anyway. I never go anywhere."

"But you're going now, Aunt Lucretia," said he, "and it does matter, you see. Clothes are easily bought. We'll go shopping after breakfast tomorrow morning."

"But I really can't afford it, Donald," said his aunt with an air of finality. "You know I'm not rich. If Carrie weren't good enough to give me a home here, I shouldn't know how to make two ends meet."

"Never mind that, Aunt Crete; this is my layout, and I'm paying for it. We'll go shopping tomorrow morning. I've got some money in my pocket I'm just aching to spend. The fact is, Aunt Crete, I struck gold up there in the Klondike, and I've got more money than I know what to do with."

"Oh!" said Aunt Crete with awe in her voice at the thought of having more money than one knew what to do with. Then shyly, "But——"

"But what, Aunt Lucretia?" asked Donald as she hesitated and flushed till the double V came into her forehead in the old helpless, worried way.

"Why, there's lots of canning and housecleaning that has got to be done, and I don't really think Carrie would like it to have me leave it all, and run away on a pleasure excursion."

Righteous indignation filled the heart of the nephew.

"Well, I should like to know why she wouldn't like it!" he exclaimed impulsively. "Has she any better right to have a vacation than you? I'm sure you've earned it. You blessed little woman, you're going to have a vacation now, in spite of yourself. Just put your conscience away in pink cotton till we get back—though I don't know whether I shall let you come back to stay. I may spirit you off with me somewhere if I don't like the looks of my cousin. I'll take all the responsibility of this trip. If Aunt Carrie doesn't like it, she may visit her wrath on me, and I'll tell her just what I think of her. Anyhow, to the shore you are going right speedily; that is, if you want to go. If there's some other place you'd rather go besides to the Traymore, speak the word, and there we'll go. I want you to have a good time."

Aunt Crete gasped with joy. The thought of the ocean, the real ocean, was wonderful. She had dreamed of it many times, but never had seen it, because she was always the one who could just as well stay at home as not. She never got run down or nervous or cross, and was ordered to go away for her health, and she never insisted upon going when the rest went. Her heart was bounding as it had not bounded since the morning of the last Sunday-school picnic she had attended when she was a girl.

"Indeed, dear boy, I do want to go with all my heart if I really ought. I have always wanted to see the ocean, and I can't imagine any place I'd rather go than the Traymore, Luella's talked so much about it."

"All right. Then it's settled that we go. How soon can we get ready? We'll go shopping tomorrow morning bright and early, and get a trunkful of new clothes. It's always nice to have new things when you go off; you feel like another person, and don't have to be sewing on buttons all the time," laughed Donald, as if he was enjoying the whole thing as much as his aunt. "I meant to have a good time getting presents for the whole family, but, as they aren't here, I'm going to get them all for you. You're not to say a word. Have you got a trunk."

"Trunk? No, child. I haven't ever had any need for a trunk. The time I went to Uncle Hiram's funeral I took Carrie's old haircloth one, but I don't know 's that's fit to travel again. Carrie's got her flannels packed away in camphor in it now, and I shouldn't like to disturb it."

"Then we'll get a trunk."

"Oh, no," protested Aunt Crete, "that would be a foolish expense. There's some pasteboard boxes upstairs. I can make out with them in a shawl strap. I shan't need much for a few days."

"Enlarge your scale of things, Aunt Crete. You're going to stay more than a few days. You're going to stay till you're tired, and just want to come back. As we're going to a 'swell' hotel"—Donald reflected that Aunt Crete could not understand his reference to Luella's description of the Traymore—"we can't think of shawl straps and boxes. You shall have a big trunk. I saw an advertisement of one that has drawers and a hatbox in it, like a bureau. We'll see if we can find one to suit."

"It sounds just like the fairy tales I used to read to Luella when she was a little girl," beamed Aunt Crete. "It doesn't seem as if it was I. I can't make it true."

"Now let's write down a list of things you need," said the eager planner, "we'll have to hurry up things, and get off this week if possible. I've been reading the paper, and they say there's coming a hot wave. I need to get you to the shore before it arrives, if possible. Come, what shall I put down first? What have you always thought you'd like, Aunt Crete? Don't you need some silk dresses?"

"Oh, dear heart! Hear him! Silk dresses aren't for me. Of course I've always had a sort of hankering after one, but nothing looks very well on me. Carrie says my figure is dumpy. I guess, if you're a mind to, you can get me a lace collar. It'll please me as well as anything. Luella saw some for a quarter that were real pretty. She bought one for herself. I think it would do to wear with my new pin, and all my collars are pretty much worn out."

"Now look here, Aunt Crete! Can't I make you understand? I mean business, and no collars for a quarter are going to do. You can have a few cheap ones for morning if you want them, but we'll buy some real lace ones to wear with the pin. And you shall have the silk dress, two or three of them, and a lot of other things. What kind do you want?"

"Oh, my dear boy! You just take my breath away. I with two or three silk dresses! The idea! Carrie would think me extravagant, and Luella wouldn't like it a bit. She always tells me I'm too gay for my years."

Donald set his lips, and wished he could have speech for a few minutes with the absent Luella. He felt that he would like to express his contempt for her treatment of their aunt.

"I've always thought I'd like a gray silk," mused Aunt Crete with a dreamy look in her eyes, "but I just know Luella would think it was too dressy for me. I suppose black would be better. I can't deny I'd like black silk, too."

"We'll have both," said Donald decidedly. "I saw a woman in a silver-gray silk once. She had white hair like yours, and the effect was beautiful. Then you'll need some other things. White dresses, I guess. That's what my chum's grandmother used to wear when I went there visiting in the summer."

"White for me!" exclaimed the aunt. "Oh, Luella would be real angry at me getting white. She says it's too conspicuous for old women to dress in light colors."

"Never mind Luella. We're doing this, and whatever we want goes. If Luella doesn't like it, she needn't look at it."

Aunt Crete was all in a flutter that night. She could hardly sleep. She did not often go to town. Luella did all the shopping. Sometimes she suggested going, but Carrie always said it was a needless expense, and, besides, Luella knew how to buy at a better bargain. It was a great delight to go with Donald. Her face shone, and all the weariness of the day's work, and all the toilsome yesterdays, disappeared from her brow.

She looked over her meager wardrobe, most of it cast-offs from Carrie's or Luella's half-worn clothing, and wrote down in a cramped hand a few absolute necessities. The next morning they had an early breakfast, and started at once on their shopping expedition. Aunt Crete felt like a little child being taken to the circus. The idea of getting a lot of new clothes all for herself seemed too serious a business to be true. She was dazed when she thought of it, and so, when Donald asked what they should look at first, she showed plainly that she would be little help in getting herself fitted out. She was far to happy to bring her mind down to practical things, and, besides, she could not adjust herself to the vast scale of expenditure Donald had set.

"Here are some collars," said Donald. "We might as well begin on those."

Aunt Crete examined them with enthusiasm, and finally picked out two at twenty-five cents apiece.

"Are those the best you have?" questioned Donald.

"Oh, no," said the saleswoman, quick to identify the purchaser that did not stop at price, "did you want real or imitation?"

"Real, by all means," he answered promptly.

"Oh, Donald," breathed Aunt Crete in a warning whisper, "real lace comes dreadful high. I've heard Luella say so. Besides, I shouldn't have anything to wear it with, nor any place to go fixed up like that."

"Have you forgotten you're going to the Traymore in a few days?" he asked her with a twinkle in his eye. "And what about the gray silk? Won't it go with that? If not, we'll get something better."

Assisted by the saleswoman, they selected two beautiful collars of real lace, and half a dozen plain ones for everyday wear.

"Couldn't you go with us?" asked Donald of the saleswoman as the purchase was concluded. "My aunt wishes to get a good many things, and neither she nor I is much used to shopping. We'd like to have your advice."

"I'm sorry; I'd like to, but I'm not allowed to leave this counter," said the woman with a kindly smile. "I'm head of this department, and they can't get along without me this morning. But they have buyers in the office just for that purpose. You go up to the desk over on the east side just beyond the rotunda, and ask for a buyer to go around with you. Get Miss Brower if you can, and tell her the head of the lace department told you to call for her. She'll tell you just what to get," and she smiled again at Aunt Crete's kindly, beaming face.

They went to the desk, and found Miss Brower, who, when she heard the message, took them smilingly under her wing. She knew that meant a good sale had been made, and there would be something in it for her. Besides, she had a kindly disposition, and did not turn up a haughty nose at Aunt Crete's dumpy little figure.

"Now, just what do you want first?" she asked brightly.

"Everything," said Donald helplessly. "We've only bought a lace collar so far, and now we want all the rest of the things to go with it. The only things we've decided on so far are two silk dresses, a black one and a silver-gray. How do we go about it to get them? Do they have them ready-made?"

"Nothing that would be quite suitable, I'm afraid, in silks. But we'll go and see what there is in stock," said the assistant with skillful eye, taking in Aunt Crete's smiling, helpless face, lovely white hair, dumpy, ill-fitted figure, and all. "There might be a gray voile that would suit her. In fact, I saw one this morning, very simple and elegant, lined with gray silk, and trimmed with lace dyed to match. It is a beauty, and just reduced this morning to thirty dollars from sixty. I believe it will fit her."

Aunt Crete gasped at the price, and looked at Donald; but he seemed pleased, and said: "That sounds good. Let's go and see it. We'll have a gray—what was it you called it—voile? Remember that name, Aunt Crete. You're going to have a gray voile. But we want the silk too. Do they make things here? We want to go away in a few days, and would like to take them with us."

"Oh, yes, they'll make anything to order; and this time of year we're not so busy. I guess you could get a 'hurry-up' order on it, and have it done in a couple of days; or it could be forwarded to you if it was not quite finished when you left."

They stepped into the elevator, and in a moment were ushered into the presence of the rare and the imported. Aunt Crete stood in a maze of delight and wonder. All this was on exhibition just for her benefit, and she was Alice in Wonderland for the hour. Donald stood back with his arms folded, and watched her with satisfaction. One thing alone was wanted to complete it. He would have liked to have Luella up in the gallery somewhere watching also. But that he held in anticipation. Luella should be made to understand that she had done wrong in underrating this sweet, patient soul.

The gray voile was entirely satisfactory to the two shoppers. Donald recognized it as the thing many women of his acquaintance wore at the receptions he had attended in university circles. Aunt Crete fingered it wistfully, and had her inward doubts whether anything so frail and lovely, like a delicate veil, would wear; but, looking at Donald's happy face, she decided not to mention it. The dress was more beautiful than anything she had ever dreamed of possessing. "But it won't fit me," she sighed as she and Miss Brower were on the way to the trying-on room where the garment was to be fitted to her. "I'm so dumpy, you know, and Luella always says it's no use to get me anything ready-made."

"Oh, the fitter will make it fit," said Miss Brower convincingly; and then, with a glance at the ample waist, whose old-fashioned lines lay meekly awry as if they were used to being put on that way and were beyond even discouragement: "Why don't you wear one of those stiffened waists? There's a new one on sale, has soft bones all around, and is real comfortable. It would make your dresses set a great deal better. If you like, I'll go get one, and you can be fitted over it. You don't like anything very tight, do you?"

"No," said Aunt Crete in a deprecatory tone, "I never could bear anything real tight. That's what puts Luella out so about me. But, if you say there's a waist that's comfortable, I should be so obliged if you'd get it. I'd be willing to pay any price not to look so dumpy."

She felt that if it took the last cent she possessed, and made all her relatives angry with her, she must have something to fit her once.

Miss Brower, thus commissioned, went away, and returned very soon with the magical waist that was to transform Miss Lucretia's "figger." If Donald could have seen his aunt's face when she was finally arrayed in the soft folds of the gray voile and was being pinned up and pinned down and pinned in and pinned out, he would have been fully repaid. Aunt Crete's ecstasy was marred only by the fact that Luella could not see her grandeur. Actually being fitted in a department store to a real imported dress! Could mortal attain higher in this mundane sphere?

When the fitting was pronounced done and Aunt Crete was about to don her discouraged shirtwaist once more, Miss Brower appeared in the doorway with a coat and skirt suit over her arm, made of fine soft black taffeta.

"Just put this on and let the gentleman see how he likes

it," she said. She had been out to talk over matters with Donald and have an understanding as to what was wanted. She had advised the taffeta coat and skirt for traveling, with an extra cloth coat for cool days. Aunt Crete, with the new dignity that consciousness of her improved figure gave her, rustled out to her nephew looking like a new woman, her face beaming.

That was a wonderful day. Aunt Crete retired again for the black taffeta to be altered a little, and yet again for a black and white dotted swiss, and a white linen suit, and a handsome black crepe de chine, and then to have the measure taken for the silver-gray silk, which the head dressmaker promised could be hurried through. They bought a black chiffon waist and some filmy, dreamy white shirtwaists, simple and plain in design, with exquisite lace simply applied, fine handmade tucks, and finer material. Miss Brower advised white linen and white lawn for morning wear at the seashore, and gave Aunt Crete confidence, telling how she had a customer, "a woman about as old as you, with just such lovely white hair," who but yesterday purchased a set of white dresses for morning wear at the seashore. This silenced the thoughts of her sister's horror at "White for you, Crete! What are you thinking of?" Never mind, she was going to have one good time, even if she had to put all her lovely finery away in a trunk afterwards, and never bring it out again, or—dreary thought—were made to cut it over for Luella sometime. Well, it might come to that, but at least she would enjoy it while it was hers.

Two white linen skirts, a handsome black cloth coat, several pairs of silk gloves, black and white, some undergarments dainty enough for a bride, a whole dozen pairs of stockings! How Aunt Crete rejoiced in those! She had been wearing stockings whose feet were cut out of old stocking legs for fifteen years. She couldn't remember when she had had a whole new pair of stockings all her own. And then two new bonnets.

All these things were acquired little by little. It was while they were in the millinery department, and Miss Brower had just set a charming black lace bonnet made on a foundation of white roses on the white hair, that Donald decided she was one of the most beautiful old ladies he had ever seen. The drapery was a fine black lace scarf, which swept around the roses and tied loosely on the breast, and it gave the quiet little woman a queenly air. She was getting used to seeing her own face in strange adornments, but it startled her to see that she really looked handsome in this bonnet. She stood before the transformation in the mirror almost in awe, and never heard what Miss Brower was saying:

"That's just the thing for best, and there's a lovely lace wrap in the cloak department she ought to have to go with it. It would be charming."

"Get it," said Donald with respectful brevity. He was astonished himself at the difference mere clothes made. Aunt Crete was fairly impressive in her new bonnet. And the lace wrap proved indeed to be the very mate to the bonnet, hiding the comfortable figure, and making her look "just like other people," as she breathlessly expressed it after one glance at herself in the lace wrap.

They bought a plain black bonnet, a sweet little gray one, a fine silk umbrella, a lot of pretty belts and handkerchiefs, some shoes and rubbers, a handbag of cut steel, for which Luella would have bartered her conscience—what there was left of it; and then they smiled good-bye at Miss Brower, and left her for a little while, and went to lunch.

Such a lunch! Soup and fish and spring lamb and fresh peas and new potatoes and two kinds of ice cream in little hard sugar cases that looked like baked snowballs. Aunt Crete's hand trembled as she took the first spoonful. The wonders of the day had been so great that she was fairly worn out, and two little bright red spots of excitement had appeared in her cheeks, but she was happy! Happier than she remembered ever to have been in her life before. Her dear old conscience had a moment of sighing that Luella could not have been there to have enjoyed it too, and then her heart bounded in wicked gleefulness that Luella was not there to stop her nice time.

They went into a great hall in the same store, and sat among the palms and coolness made by electric fans, while a wonderful organ played exquisite music, and Aunt Crete felt she certainly was in heaven without the trouble of dying; and she never dreamed, dear soul, that she had been dying all her life that others might live, and that it is to such that the reward is promised.

They went back to Miss Brower later; and behold! the silver-gray silk had been cut out, and was ready to fit. Aunt Crete felt it was fairy work, the whole of it, and she touched the fabric as if it had been made by magic.

Then they went and bought a trunk and a handsome leather satchel, and Donald took a notion that his aunt must have a set of silver combs for her hair such as he saw in the hair of another old lady.

"Now," said Donald reflectively, "we'll go home and get

rested, and tomorrow we'll come down and buy any things we've forgotten."

"And I'm sure I don't see what more a body could possibly need," said Aunt Crete, as, tired and absolutely contented, she climbed into the train and sat down in the hot plush seat.

The one bitter drop in the cup of bliss came the next morning—or rather two drops—in the shape of letters. One from Aunt Carrie for Donald was couched in stiffest terms, in which she professed to have just heard of his coming, and to be exceedingly sorry that she was not at home, and was kept from returning only by a sprained ankle, the doctor telling her that she must not put her foot to the ground for two or three weeks yet, or she would have to suffer for it.

The other letter was for Aunt Crete, and was a rehash of the telephone message, with a good sound scolding for having gone away from the telephone before she finished speaking. Luella had written it herself because she felt like venting her temper on someone. The young man that had been so attentive to her in town had promenaded the piazza with another young woman all the evening before. Luella hoped Aunt Crete would put up plenty of gooseberry jam. Aunt Crete put on her double V as she read, and sighed for a full minute before Donald looked up amused from his letter.

"Now, Aunt Crete, you look as if a mountain had rolled down upon you. What's the matter?"

"Oh, I'm just afraid, Donald, that I'm doing wrong going off this way, when Carrie expects me to do all this canning and sewing and cleaning. I'm afraid she'll never forgive me."

"Now, Aunt Crete, don't you love me? Didn't I tell you I'd stand between you and the whole world? Please put that letter up, and come and help me pack your new trunk. Do you want that gray silk put in first, or shall I put the shoes at the bottom? Don't you know you and I are going to have the time of our lives? We're going to run away from every care. Do you suppose your own sister would want you to stay here roasting in the city if she knew you had a nephew just aching to carry you off to the ocean? Come, forget it. Cut it out, Aunt Crete, and let's pack the trunk. I'm longing to be off to smell the briny deep." And laughingly he carried her away, and plunged her into thoughts of her journey, giving her no time the rest of the day to think of anything else.

Chapter 4

Aunt Crete Transformed

They locked the house early one morning when even the dusty bricks had a smell of freshness to them before the hot sun baked them for another day. The closed blinds seemed sullen like a conquered tyrant, and the front door looked reproachfully at Aunt Crete as she turned the key carefully and tried it twice to be sure it was locked. The lonesome look of the house gave the poor old lady a pang as she turned the corner in her softly rustling silk coat and skirt. She felt it had hardly been right to put on a new black silk in the morning, and go off from all the cares of the world, just leave them, boldly ignore them, like any giddy girl, and take a vacation. She regarded herself with awe and a rising self-respect in every window she passed. Somehow the look of dumpiness had passed away mysteriously. It was not her old self that was passing along the street to the station bearing a cut-steel handbag, while Donald carried her new satchel, and her new trunk bumped on a square ahead in the expressman's wagon.

It was a hot morning, and the great city station seemed close and stuffy, but Aunt Crete mingled with the steaming crowd blissfully. To be one with the world, attired irreproachably; to be on her way to a great hotel by the sea, with new clothes, and escorted devotedly by someone who was her very own, this indeed was happiness. Could anyone desire more upon the earth?

Donald put her into a cab at the station, and she beamed happily out at the frightful streets that always made her heart come into her mouth on the rare occasions when she had to cross them. The ride across the city seemed a brief and distinguished experience. It was as if everybody else was walking and they only had the grandeur of a carriage. Then the ferry boat was delightful to the new traveler, with its long, white-ceiled passages, and its smell of wet timbers and tarred ropes. They had a seat close to the front, where they could look out and watch their own progress and see the many puffing monsters laboriously plying back and forth, and the horizon line of many masts, like fine brown lines against the sky. Aunt Crete felt that at last she was out in the world. She could not have felt it more if she had been starting for Europe.

The seashore train, with its bamboo seats and its excited groups of children bearing tin pails and shovels and tennis-rackets, filled her with a fine exhilaration. At last, at last, her soul had escaped the bounds of red brick walls that she had expected would surround her as long as she lived. She drew deep breaths, and beamed upon the whole trainful of people, yelling baby and all. She gazed and gazed at the fast-flying Jersey scenery, grown so monotonous to some of the travelers, and admired every little white and green town at which they paused.

Donald put her into a carriage when they reached the shore. Half an hour off they had begun to smell the sea, and to catch glimpses of low-lying marshes and a misty blueness against the sky. Now every friendly hackman at the station seemed a part of the great day to Aunt Crete. So pretty a carriage, with low steps and gray cushions and a fringe all around the canopy, and a white speckled horse, with long, gentle, white eyelashes. Aunt Crete leaned back self-consciously on the gray cushions, and enjoyed the creak of her silk jacket as she settled into place. She felt as if this was a play that would soon be over; but she would enjoy it to the very end, and then go back to her dishwashing and cellar-cleaning, and being blamed, and bear them all in happy remembrance of what she had had for one blissful vacation.

She did not know that Donald had telephoned ahead for the best apartments in the hotel. She was engaged in watching for the first blue line of the great mysterious ocean; and, when it came into sight, billowing suddenly above the line of boardwalk as they turned a corner, her heart stood still for one moment, and then bounded onward set to the time of wonder.

Two obsequious porters jumped to assist Aunt Crete from the carriage. The hand baggage drifted up the steps as if by magic, and awaited them in the apartments to which they arose in a luxurious elevator. Aunt Crete noticed several old ladies with pink and blue wool knitting, sitting in a row of large rocking chairs, as she glided up to the second floor. It gave her rest on one point, for they all wore white dresses. She had been a little dubious about those white dresses that Donald had insisted upon. But now she might enjoy them unashamed. Oh, what would Luella say?

She glanced around the room, half-fearfully expecting to find Luella waiting there. Somehow, now she was there, she wanted to get used to it and enjoy it all before Luella came. For Luella was an uncertain quantity. Luella might not like it, after all! Dreadful thought! And after Donald had taken so much trouble and spent so much money all to surprise them!

The smiling porter absorbed the goodly tip that Donald handed him, and went his way. Aunt Crete and Donald were left alone. They looked at each other and smiled.

"Let's look around and see where they've put us," said Donald, pushing the swaying curtains aside, and there before them rolled the blue tide of the ocean. Aunt Crete sank into a chair, and was silent for a while; and then she said: "It's just as big as I thought it would be. I was so afraid it wouldn't be. Some folks next door went down to the shore last year, and they said it didn't look big enough to what they'd expected, and I've been afraid ever since."

Donald's eyes filled with a tender light that was beautiful to see. He was enjoying the spending of his money, and it was yielding him a rich reward already.

The apartments that had been assigned to them consisted of a parlor and two large bedrooms with private baths. Donald discovered a few moments later, when he went down to the office to investigate, that Luella and his aunt occupied a single room on the fourth floor back, overlooking the kitchen court. It was not where he would have placed them, had they chosen to await his coming and be taken down to the shore in style. But now that they had run away from him, and were too evidently ashamed of him, perhaps it was as well to let them remain where they were, he reflected.

"Aunt Carrie and Luella have gone out with a party in a carriage for an all-day drive to Pleasure Bay," announced

Donald when he came up. "Aunt Carrie's ankle must be better."

"Well, that's real nice!" exclaimed Aunt Crete with a smile, turning from her view of the sea, where she had been ever since he left her. "I'm glad Luella is having a good time, and we shan't miss her a mite. You and I'll have the ocean all to ourselves today."

Donald smiled approvingly. He was not altogether sure he cared to meet that other aunt and cousin at all. He was not sure but he would like to run away from them, and carry Aunt Crete with him.

"Very well," he said, "I'm glad you're not disappointed. We'll do just whatever we want to. Would you like to go in bathing?"

"Oh, my! Could I! I've always thought I'd like to see how it would feel, but I guess I'm too old. Besides, there's my figger. It wouldn't look nice in a bathing suit. Luella wouldn't like it a bit, and I don't want to disgrace her, now I'm here. She always makes a lot of fun of old people going in and sitting right on the edge of the water. I guess it won't do."

"Yes, it will do, if you want to. Didn't I tell you this was my party, and Luella isn't in it? That's ridiculous. I'll take you in myself, Aunt Crete, and we'll have the best time out; and you shan't be scared, either. I can swim like a fish. You shall go in every day. Would you like to begin at once?"

"I should," said Aunt Crete, rising with a look of resolution in her face. She felt that Luella would condemn the amusement for her; so, if she was to dare it, it must be done before her niece appeared.

They went down to the beach, and for a few minutes surveyed the bathers as they came out to the water. Then with

joy and daring in her face Aunt Crete went into the little
bathhouse with wildly beating heart, arrayed herself in the
gay blue flannel garb provided for her use, and came timidly
out to meet Donald, tall and smiling in his blue jerseys.

They had a wonderful time. It was almost better than
shopping. Donald led her down to the water, and very
gently accustomed her to it until he had led her out beyond
the roughness, where his strong arms lifted her well above
the swells until she felt as if she was a bird. It was marvelous
that she was not afraid, but she was not. It was as if she had
that morning been transferred back over forty years to her
youth again, and was having the good times that she had
longed for, such as other girls had—the swings and the rides
and the skatings and bicyclings. How many such things she
had watched through the years, with her heart palpitating
with daring to do it all herself! Her petulant sister and the
logy Luella never dreamed that Aunt Crete desired such un-
auntly indulgences. If they had, they would have taken it
out of her, scorched it out with scorn.

The white hair with its natural waves fluffed out beautifully, like a canary's feathers, after the bath, and Aunt Crete
was smiling and charming at lunch in one of her fine new
white dresses. She had hurried to put it on before Luella appeared, lest they might all be spirited away from her if
Luella discovered them. She reflected with a sigh that they
would likely fit Luella beautifully, and that that would probably be their final destination, just as Luella's discarded
garments came to her.

But there was nothing to mar the lunchtime and the
beautiful afternoon, wherein, after a delicious nap to the ac-
companiment of the music of the waves, she was taken to

drive in the fringed carriage again, while a bunch of handsome ladies, old and young, sat on the hotel piazza in more of those abundant rockers, and watched her approvingly. She felt that she was of some importance in their eyes. She had suddenly blossomed out of her insignificance, and was worth looking at. It warmed her heart with humble pleasure. She felt that she had won approval, not through any merit of her own, but through Donald's loving-kindness. It was wonderful what a charm clothes could work.

"Put on your gray silk for dinner," said Donald with malice aforethought in his heart.

"Oh," gasped Aunt Crete, "I think I ought to keep that for parties, don't you?"

"If ever there was a party, it's going to be tonight," said Donald. "It's going to be a surprise-party. You want to see if Aunt Carrie and Luella will know you, you know."

So with trembling fingers Aunt Crete arrayed herself in her gray silk and fine linen, very materially assisted by a quiet maid, whom Donald had ordered sent to the room, and who persuaded Aunt Crete to let her arrange the pretty white hair.

It was surprising to see, when the coiffure was complete, that she looked quite like the other old ladies, who were not old at all, only playing old.

"I don't believe they will know me," whispered Aunt Crete to herself as she stood before the full-length mirror and surveyed the effect. "And I didn't think I could ever look like that!" she murmured after a more prolonged gaze, during which she made the acquaintance of her new self. Then she added half wistfully: "I wish I had known it before. I think perhaps they'd have—liked me—more if I'd looked that way all the time." She sighed half regretfully, as if she were bidding good-bye to this new vision, and went out to Donald, who awaited her. She felt that the picnic part of her vacation was almost over now, for Carrie and Luella would be sure to manage to spoil it someway.

Donald looked up from his paper with a welcome in his eyes. It was the first time she had seen him in evening dress, and she thought him handsome as a king.

"You're a very beautiful woman, Aunt Crete; do you know it?" said Donald with satisfaction. He had felt that the French maid would know how to put just the right touch to Aunt Crete's pretty hair to take away her odd "unused" appearance. Now she was completely in fashion, and she looked every inch a lady. She somehow seemed to have natural intuition for gentle manners. Perhaps her kindly heart dictated them, for surely there can be no better manners than come wrapped up with the Golden Rule, and Aunt Crete had lived by that all her life.

They entered the great dining hall, and made their way among the palms in a blaze of electric light, with the head-waiter bowing obsequiously before them. They had a table to themselves, and Aunt Crete rejoiced in the tiny shaded candles and the hothouse roses in the center, and lifted the handsome napkins and silver forks with awe. Sometimes it seemed as if she were still dreaming.

The party from Pleasure Bay had reached home rather late in the afternoon, after a tedious time in the hot sun at a place full of peanut stands and merry-go-rounds and moving picture shows. Luella had not had a good time. She had been disappointed that none of the young men in the party had paid her special attention. In fact, the special young man for whose sake she had prodded her mother into going had not accompanied them at all. Luella was thoroughly cross.

"Mercy, how you've burned your nose, Luella!" said her mother sharply. "It's so unbecoming. The skin is all peeling off. I do wish you'd wear a veil. You can't afford to lose your complexion, with such a figure as you have."

"Oh, fiddlesticks! I wish you'd let up on that, Ma," snapped Luella. "Didn't you get a letter from Aunt Crete? I wonder what she's thinking about not to send that lavender organdie. I wanted to wear it tonight. There's to be a hop in the ballroom, and that would be just the thing. She ought to have got it done; she's had time enough since I telephoned. I suppose she's gone to reading again. I do wish I'd remembered to lock up the bookcase. She's crazy for novels."

All this time Luella was being buttoned into a pink silk muslin heavily decorated with cheap lace. There were twenty-six tiny elusive buttons, and Luella's mother was tired.

"What on earth makes you so long, Ma?" snarled Luella, twisting her neck to try to see her back. "We'll be so late we won't get served, and I'm hungry as a bear."

They hurried down, arriving at the door just as Aunt Crete and Donald were being settled into their chairs by the smiling headwaiter.

"For goodness' sake! those must be swells," said Luella in a low tone. "Did you see how that waiter bowed and smiled? He never does that to us. I expect he got a big tip. See, they're sitting right next to our table. Goodness, Ma, your hair is all slipped to one side. Put it up quick. No, the other side. Say, he's an awfully handsome young man. I wonder if we can get introduced. I just know he dances gracefully. Say, Mother, I'd like to get him for a partner tonight. I guess those stuck-up Grandons would open their eyes then."

"Hush, Luella, he'll hear you."

They settled into their places unassisted by the dilatory waiter, who came languidly up a moment later to take their order.

Aunt Crete's back was happily toward her relatives, so she ate her dinner in comfort. The palms were all about, and the gentle clink of silver and glass, and refined voices. The soft strains of an orchestra hidden in a balcony of ferns and palms drowned Luella's strident voice when it was raised in discontented strain, and so Aunt Crete failed to recognize the sound. But Donald had been on the alert. In the first place, he had asked a question or two, and knew about where his relatives usually sat, and had purposely asked to be placed near them. He studied Luella when she came in, and felt pretty sure she was the girl he had seen on the platform of the train the morning he arrived in Midvale; and finally in a break in the music he distinctly caught the name "Luella" from the lips of the sour woman in the purple satin with white question-marks all over it and plasters of white lace.

Aunt Carrie was tall and thin, with a discontented droop to her lips, and premature wrinkles. She wore an affected air of abnormal politeness and disapproval of everything. She was studying the silver-gray silk back in front of her and wondering what there was about that elegant-looking woman with the lovely white waved pompadour and puffs, and that exquisite real lace collar, to remind her of poor sister Lucretia. She always coupled the adjective "poor" with her sister's name when she thought of all her shortcomings.

Luella's discontent was somewhat enlivened by the sight of the young man that had not gone on the drive to Pleasure Bay. He stood in the doorway, searching the room with keen, interested eyes. Could it be that he was looking for her? Luella's heart leaped in a moment's triumph. Yes, he seemed to be looking that way as if he had found the object of his search, and he was surely coming down toward them with a real smile on his face. Luella's face broke into preparatory smiles. She would be very coy, and pretend not to see him, so she began a voluble and animated conversation with her mother about the charming time they had had that day, which might have surprised the worthy woman if she had not been accustomed to her daughter's wiles. She knew it to be a warning of the proximity of someone that Luella wished to charm.

The young man came on straight by the solicitous waiters, who waved him frantically to various tables. Luella cast a rapid side glance, and talked on gayly with drooping head and averted gaze. Her mother looked up, wondering, to see what was the cause of Luella's animation. He was quite near now, and in a moment more he would speak. The girl felt excited thrills creeping up her back, and the color rushed into her cheeks, which were already red enough from the wind and sun of the day.

"Well, well," said the young man's voice in a hearty eagerness Luella had never hoped to hear addressed to herself, "this is too good to be true. Don, old man, where did you drop from? I saw your name in the register, and rushed right into the dining room——"

"Clarence Grandon, as true as I live!" said a pleasant

voice behind Luella. "I thought you were in Europe, bless your heart. This is the best thing that could have happened. Let me introduce my aunt——"

Some seconds before this Luella's thrills had changed to chills. Mortification stole over her face and up to the roots of her hair. Even the back of her neck, where her bathing suit was cut low and square, turned angry looking. The pink muslin had a round neck, and showed a half-circle of whiter neck below the bathing suit square. But Luella had the presence of mind to smile on to her mother in mild pretense that she had but just noticed the advent of the young man behind. An obsequious waiter was bringing an extra chair for Mr. Grandon, and he was to be seated so that he could look toward their table. Perhaps he would recognize her yet, and there might be a chance of introduction to the handsome stranger. Luella dallied with her dinner in fond hope, and her mother aided and abetted her.

The lovely old lady with the silver-gray silk and the real lace collar and beautiful hair had her back squarely toward the table where Luella and her mother sat. They could not see her face. They could only notice how interested both the young men were in her, and how courteous they were to her, and they decided she must be some very great personage indeed. They watched her half enviously, and began to plan some way to scrape an acquaintance with her. One glimpse they had of her face as the headwaiter rushed to draw back her chair when she had finished her dinner. It was a fine, handsome face, younger than they had expected to see, with beautiful sparkling eyes full of mirth and contentment. What was there in the face that reminded them of something? Had they ever met that old lady before?

Luella and her mother brought their dallied dessert to a sudden ending, and followed hard upon the footsteps of the three down the length of the dining hall; but the lady in gray and her two attendants had disappeared already, and disconsolately they lingered about, looking up and down the length of piazzas in vain hope to see them sitting in one of the great rows of rockers, watching the many-tinted waves in the dying evening light, but there was no sign of them anywhere.

As they stood thus leaning over the balcony, a large automobile, gray, with white cushions, like a great gliding dove, slipped silently up to the entrance below them in the well-bred silence that an expensive machine knows how to assume under dignified owners.

Luella twitched her mother's sleeve. "That's Grandon's car," she whispered. "P'raps I'll get asked to go. Let's sit down here and wait."

The mother obediently sat down.

Chapter 5

Luella and Her Mother Are Mystified

They had not long to wait. They heard the elevator door slide softly open, and then the gentle swish of silken skirts. Luella looked around just in time to be recognized by young Mr. Grandon if he had not at that moment been placing a long white broadcloth coat about his mother's shoulders. There were four in the party, and Luella's heart sank. He would not be likely to ask another one. The young man and the gray-silk, thread-lace woman from the other dining table were going with them, it appeared. Young Mr. Grandon helped the gray-silk lady down the steps while the handsome stranger walked by Mrs. Grandon. They did not look around at the people on the piazza at all. Luella bit her lips in vexation.

"For pity's sake, Luella, don't scowl so," whispered her mother; "they might look up yet and see you."

This warning came just in time; for young Mr. Grandon just as he was about to start the car glanced up, and, catching Luella's fixed gaze, gave her a distant bow, which was followed by a courteous lifting of the stranger's hat.

Aunt Crete was seated beside Mrs. Grandon in the back seat and beaming her joy quietly. She was secretly exulting

that Luella and Carrie had not been in evidence yet. She felt
that her joy was being lengthened by a few minutes more,
for she could not get away from the fear that her sister and
niece would spoil it all as soon as they appeared upon the
scene.

"I thought Aunt Carrie and Luella would be tired after
their all-day trip, and we wouldn't disturb them tonight,"
said Donald in a low tone, looking back to Aunt Crete as the
car glided smoothly out from the shelter of the wide piazza.

Aunt Crete smiled happily back to Donald, and raised her
eyes with a relieved glance toward the rows of people on the
piazza. She had been afraid to look her fill before lest she
should see Luella frowning at her somewhere; but evidently
they had not got back yet, or perhaps had not finished their
dinner.

As Aunt Crete raised her eyes, Luella and her mother
looked down into her upturned face enviously, but Aunt
Crete's gaze had but just grazed them and fallen upon an old
lady of stately mien with white, fluffy hair like her own, and
a white crepe de chine gown trimmed with much white lace.
In deep satisfaction Aunt Crete reflected that, if Luella had
aught to say against her aunt's wearing modest white morning gowns, she would cite this model, who was evidently an
old aristocrat if one might judge by her jewels and her gen-
eral makeup.

"Somewhere I've seen that woman with the gray silk!"
exclaimed Luella's mother suddenly as Aunt Crete swept by.
"There's something real familiar about the set of her shoulders. Look at the way she raises her hand to her face. My
land! I believe she reminds me of your Aunt Crete!"

"Now, Mother!" scorned Luella. "As if Aunt Crete could

ever look like that! You must be crazy to see anything in
such an elegant lady to remind you of poor old Aunt Crete.
Why, Ma, this woman is the real thing! Just see how her
hair's put up. Nobody but a French maid could get it like
that. Imagine Aunt Crete with a French maid. Oh, I'd die
laughing. She's probably washing our country cousin's sup-
per dishes at this very minute. I wonder if her conscience
doesn't hurt her about my lavender organdie. Say, Ma, did
you notice how graceful that handsome stranger was when
he handed the ladies into the car? My, but I'd like to know
him. I think Clarence Grandon is just a stuck-up prig."

Her mother looked at her sharply.

"Luella, seems to me you change your mind a good deal.
If I don't make any mistake, you came down here so's to be
near him. What's made you change your mind? He doesn't
seem to go with any other girls."

"No, he just sticks by his mother every living minute,"
sighed Luella unhappily. "I do wish I had that lavender organdie. I look better in that than anything else I've got. I
declare I think Aunt Crete is real mean and selfish not to
send it. I'm going in to see if the mail has come; and, if the
organdie isn't here, nor any word from Aunt Crete, I'm
going to call her up on the telephone again."

Luella vanished into the hotel office, and her mother sat
and rocked with puckered brows. She very much desired a
place in high society for Luella, but how to attain it was the
problem. She had not been born for social climbing, and
found it difficult to do.

Meantime the motorcar rolled smoothly over the perfect
roads, keeping always that wonderful gleaming sea in sight;
and Aunt Crete, serenely happy, beamed and nodded to the

pleasant chat of Mrs. Grandon, and was so overpowered by
her surroundings that she forgot to be overpowered by the
grand Mrs. Grandon. As in a dream she heard the kindly
tone, and responded mechanically to the questions about
her journey and the weather in the city, and how lovely the
sea was tonight; but, as she spoke the few words with her
lips, her soul was singing, and the words of its song were
these:

> Must I be carried to the skies
>   On flowery beds of ease,
> While others fought to win the prize
>   And sailed through bloody seas?

And it seemed to her as they glided along the palace-lined
shore, with the rolling sea on one hand, and the beautiful
people in their beautiful raiment at ease and happy on the
other hand, that she was picked right up out of the hot little
brick house in the narrow street, and put on a wonderfully
flowery bed of ease, and was floating right into a heaven of
which her precious Donald was a bright, particular angel.
She forgot all about Luella and what she might say, and just
enjoyed herself.

She even found herself telling the elegant Mrs. Grandon
exactly how she made piccalilli, and her heart warmed to the
other woman as she saw that she was really interested. She
had never supposed, from the way in which Luella spoke of
the Grandons, that they would even deign to eat such a
common thing as a pickle, let alone knowing anything about
it. Aunt Crete's decision was that Mrs. Grandon wasn't
stuck-up in the least, but just a nice, common lady like anyone; and, as she went up in the elevator beside her, and said

good-night, she felt as if she had known her all her life.

It was not until she had turned out her light and crept into the great hotel bed that it came to her to wonder whether Luella and Carrie could be meant by the ones in the hymn,

> While others fought to win the prize
> And sailed through bloody seas.

She couldn't help feeling that perhaps she had been selfish in enjoying her day so much when for aught she knew Luella might not be having a good time. For Luella not to have a good time meant blame for her aunt generally. Ever since Luella had been born it had been borne in upon Aunt Crete that there was a moral obligation upon her to make Luella have a good time. And now Aunt Crete was having a good time, the time of her life; and she hugged herself, she was so happy over it, and thought of the dear stars out there in the deep, dark blue of the arching sky, and the cool, dark roll of the white-tipped waves, and was thankful.

Luella and her mother had gloomily watched the dancing through the open windows of the ballroom; but, as they knew no one inside, they did not venture in. Luella kept one eye out for the return of the car, but somehow missed it, and finally retired to the solace of cold cream and the comforts of the fourth floor back, where lingered in the atmosphere a reminder of the dinner past and a hint of the breakfast that was to come.

As the elevator ascended past the second floor, the door of one of the special apartments stood wide, revealing a glimpse of the handsome young stranger standing under the chandelier reading a letter, his face alive with pleasure. Luella sighed enviously, and in her dreams strove vainly to enter into the charmed circle where these favored beings moved, and knew not that of her own free will she had closed the door to that very special apartment, which might have been hers but for her own action.

The next morning Luella was twisting her neck in a vain endeavor to set the string of artificial puffs straight upon the enormous cushion of her hair, till they looked for all the world like a pan of rolls just out of the oven. She had jerked them off four separate times, and pulled the rest of her hair down twice in a vain attempt to get just the desired effect; and her patience, never very great at any time, was well-nigh exhausted. Her mother was fretting because the best pieces of fish and all the hot rolls would be gone before they got down to breakfast, and Luella was snapping back in most undaughterly fashion, when a noticeable tap came on the door. It was not the tap of the chambermaid of the fourth floor back, nor of the elevator boy, who knew how to modulate his knock for every grade of room from the second story, ocean front, up and back. It was a knock of rare condescension, mingled with a call to attention; and it warned these favored occupants of room 410 to sit up and take notice, not that they were worthy of any such consideration as was about to fall upon them.

Luella drove the last hairpin into the puffs, and sprang to the door just as her mother opened it. She felt something was about to happen. Could it be that she was to be invited to ride in that automobile at last, or what?

There in the hall, looking very much out of place, and as if he hoped his condescension would be appreciated, but he doubted it, stood the uniformed functionary who usually confined his activities to the second floor front, where the tips were large and the guests of unquestioned wealth, to say nothing of culture. He held in his hand a shining silver tray on which lay two cards, and he delivered his message in a tone that not only showed the deference he felt for the one who had sent him, but compelled such deference also on the part of those to whom he spoke.

"The lady and gen'leman say, Will the ladies come down to the private pahlah as soon aftah breakfus' as is convenient, room number 2, second floor front?" He bowed to signify that his mission was completed, and that if it did not carry through, it was entirely beyond his sphere to do more.

Luella grasped the cards and smothered an exclamation of delight. "Second floor, front," gasped her mother. "The private parlor! Did you hear, Luella?"

But Luella was standing by the one window, frowning over the cards. One was written and one engraved, a lady's and a gentleman's cards. "Miss Ward." "Mr. Donald Ward Grant."

"For the land's sake, Ma! Who in life are they? Do you know any Miss Ward? You don't s'pose it's that lovely gray-silk woman. Miss Ward. Donald Ward Grant. Who can they be, and what do you suppppose they want? Grant. Donald Grant. Where have I, why—! Oh, horrors, Ma! It can't be that dreadful cousin has followed us up, can it? Donald Grant is his name, of course; yes, Donald Ward Grant. It was the Ward that threw me off. But who is the other? Miss Ward. Ma! You don't——!"

"Luella Burton, that's just what it is! It's your Aunt Crete and that dreadful cousin. Crete never did have any sense, if she is my sister. But just let me get ahold of her! If I don't make her writhe. I think I'll find a way to make her under-stand——"

Luella's expansive bravery beneath the row of biscuit puffs seemed to shrink and cringe as she took in the thought.

"Oh, Ma!" she groaned. "How could she? And here of all places! To come here and mortify me! It is just too dreadful. Ma, it can't be true. Aunt Crete would never dare. And where would she get the money? She hasn't a cent of her own, has she? You didn't go and leave her money, did you?"

"No, only a little change in my old pocketbook; it wouldn't have been enough to come down here on, unless she bought a day excursion. Wait. I did leave five dollars to pay the grocery bill with. But Crete surely wouldn't take that. Still, there's no telling. She always was a kind of a child. Oh, dear! What shall we do?" The mother sat down on the tumbled bed beside the tray of Luella's cheap trunk.

"Well, we must do something, that's certain, if we have to run away again. It would never do to have those two appear here now. Mercy! think of Aunt Crete in her old black and white silk sitting next table to that lovely lady in gray. I should simply sink through the floor."

"We can't run away, Luella," snapped the practical mother. "We've paid for our room two weeks ahead. I didn't want to do that; but you thought if Aunt Crete should get any nonsense into her head about our coming home, we could tell we'd paid for the room, and that would settle it with her. So now it's done, and we can't afford not to abide by it. Besides, what good would that do? We couldn't afford to go anywhere but home, and that would be as bad as it was in the first place. We've got to think it out. If I just had hold of Crete a minute, I'd make her fix it up. She'd have to think of some way out of it herself without any of my help, to pay her for her stupidity in coming. I can't understand how she'd do it."

"I didn't think she'd dare!" glared Luella with no pleasant expression on her face.

"I'll tell you what we'll have to do, Luella," said her mother. "We'll slip down those stairs in the back hall. I went down one day, and they go right out on the piazza that runs in front of the dining room. We'll just slip in the back door, and get our breakfast right away. It's getting pretty late. You better hurry. They've likely come up from town on that very early train, and they'll sit and wait for us. We'll ring for a messenger bellboy, and send down a note that my ankle is so much worse I can't come downstairs, and you can't leave me. We'll say: 'Mrs. Burton and Miss Burton regret that they cannot come down as requested: but Mrs. Burton is confined to her bed by a sprained ankle, and her daughter cannot leave her. Miss Ward will have to come up.' You write it on one of your visiting cards, Luella, and we'll send it down as quick as we get back from breakfast. Hurry up. The only thing about it will be that climb up three flights after breakfast, but it won't do for us to risk the elevator. Crete might recognize us, for the elevator goes right by that second floor front parlor. What I don't understand is how they got in there. It's only rich people can afford that. But, land! Crete's just like a baby; hasn't been out in the world ever; and very likely she never asked how much the rooms were, but just took the best she could lay eyes on. Or more likely it's a mistake, and she's sitting in that little reception room down on the office floor, and thinks it the second floor because she came up such a long flight of steps from the sidewalk. We'll have to tell the bellboy to hunt up the fellow that brought up their cards, and take it to the same folks. Come on now, Luella, and go slow when you turn corners. There's no telling but they might be prowling round trying to hunt us; so keep a lookout."

Thus by devious and back ways they descended to a late breakfast, and scuttled up again without being molested.

Luella wrote the note on her card as her mother dictated, and a small boy all brass buttons was despatched with careful directions; and then the two retired behind their ramparts, and waited.

Time went by, until half an hour had elapsed since they came back from breakfast. They had listened anxiously to every footfall in the hall, and part of the time Luella kept the door open a crack with her ear to it. Their nerves were all in a quiver. When the chambermaid arrived, they were fairly feverish to get her out of the way. If Aunt Crete should come while she was in the room, it might get all over the hotel what kind of relatives they had.

Mrs. Burton suggested to the chambermaid that she leave their room till last, as they wanted to write some letters before going out; but the maid declared she must do the room at once or not at all. The elevator slid up and down around the corner in the next hall. They heard a footfall now and then, but none that sounded like Aunt Crete's. They rang again for the office-boy, who declared he had delivered the message in the second floor, front, and that the lady and gentleman were both in and said, "All right." He vanished impudently without waiting for Luella's probing questions, and they looked at each other in anxiety and indignation.

"It is too mean, Ma, to lose this whole morning. I wanted

to go in bathing," complained Luella, "and now no telling how long I'll have to stick in this dull room. I wish Aunt Crete was in Halifax. Why couldn't I have had some nice relatives like that lovely old gray-silk lady and her son?"

Just then the elevator clanged open and shut, and steps came down the hall. It certainly was not Aunt Crete. Luella flew to the door at the first tap; and there, submerged in a sheaf of American Beauty roses, stood the functionary from the lower floor, with a less pompous manner than he had worn before. The roses had caused his respect for the occupants of the fourth floor, back, to rise several degrees.

Luella stood speechless in wonder, looking first at the roses and then at the servant. Such roses had never come into her life before. Could it be—must it be—but a miserable mistake?

Then the servant spoke.

"Miss Ward sends the flowers, an' is sorry the ladies aren't well. She sends her regrets, an' says she can't come to see the ladies 'count of a drive she'd promised to take today, in which she'd hoped to have the ladies' comp'ny. She hopes the ladies are better this even'n'."

He was gone, and the mother and daughter faced each other over the roses, bewilderment and awe in their faces.

"*What* did he say, Luella? *Who* sent those roses? Miss *Ward?* Luella, there's some mistake. Aunt Crete couldn't have sent them. She wouldn't *dare!* Besides, where would she get the money? It's perfectly impossible. It can't be Aunt Crete, after all. It must be someone else with the same name. Perhaps Donald has picked up someone here in the hotel; you can't tell; or perhaps it isn't our Donald at all. It's likely there's other Donald Grants in the world. What we ought to have done was to go down at once and find out, and not skulk in a corner. But you're always in such a hurry to do something, Luella. There's no telling at all who this is now. It might be those folks you admired so much, though what on earth they should have sent their cards to us for—and those lovely roses—I'm sure I don't know."

"Now, Ma, you needn't blame me. It was you proposed sending that note down; you know it was, Mother; and of course I had to do what you said. I was so upset, anyway; I didn't know what was what. But now, you see, perhaps you've cut me out of a lovely day. We might have gone on a ride with them."

"Luella," her mother broke in sharply, "if you talk another word like that, I'll take the next train back home. You don't know what you are talking about. It may be Aunt Crete, after all, and a country cousin for all you know; and, if it is, would you have wanted to go driving in the face of the whole hotel, with like as not some old shin-and-bones horse and broken-down carriage?"

Luella was silenced for the time, and the room settled into gloomy meditation.

Chapter 6

An Embarrassing Meeting

Meantime Aunt Crete in the whitest of her white was settling herself comfortably on the gray cushions of the fringed phaeton again, relief and joy mingled in her countenance. It was not that she was glad that Carrie's ankle was so bad, but that she was to have another short reprieve before her pleasure was cut off. Soon enough, she thought, would she be destined to sit in the darkened room and minister to her fussy sister, while Luella took her place in the carriages and automobiles with her handsome young cousin, as young folks should do, of course; but Oh, it was good, good, that a tired old lady, who had worked hard all her life, could yet have had this bit of a glimpse of the brighter side of life before she died.

It would be something to sit and think over as she scraped potatoes for dinner, or picked over blackberries for jam, or patiently sewed on Val lace for Luella. It would be an event to date from, and she could fancy herself mildly saying to Mrs. Judge Waters, when she sat beside her sometime at missionary meeting, if she ever did again, "When my nephew took me down to the shore," and so forth. She never knew just what to talk about when she sat beside Mrs. Judge

Waters, but here was a topic worth laying before such a great lady.

Well, it was something to be thankful for, and she resolved she just would not think of poor Carrie and Luella until her beautiful morning was over. Then she would show such patience and gratitude as would fully make up to them for her one more day of pleasure.

It was Donald, of course, who had suggested the roses. When the message came from the fourth floor back, Aunt Crete had turned white about the mouth, and her eyes had taken on a frightened, hunted look, while the double V in her forehead flashed into sight for the first time since they had reached the Atlantic coast. He saw at once in what terror Aunt Crete held her sister and niece, and his indignation arose in true Christian fashion. He resolved to place some nice hot coals on the heads of his unpleasant relatives, and run away with dear Aunt Crete again; hence the roses and the message, and Aunt Crete was fairly childish with pleasure over them when he finally persuaded her that it would be all right to send these in place of going up herself as she had been bidden.

She listened eagerly as Donald gave careful directions for the message, and the stately functionary respectfully repeated the words with his own high-sounding inflection. It made the pink come and go again in Aunt Crete's cheeks, and she felt that Luella and Carrie could not be angry with her after these roses, and especially when everything was being done up in so nice, stylish a manner.

The drive was one long dream of bliss to Aunt Crete. They went miles up the coast, and took lunch at a hotel much grander than the one they had left, so that when they

returned in the afternoon Aunt Crete felt much less in awe
of the Traymore, her experience in hotels having broadened.
They also met some friends of Donald's, a professor from
his alma mater, who with his wife was just returning from a
trip to Europe.

The bathers were making merry in the waves as they returned, and Aunt Crete's wistful look made Donald ask
whether she felt too tired to take another dip, but she declared she was not one bit tired.

She came from her bath with shining eyes and triumphant
mien. Whatever happened now, she had been in bathing
twice. She felt like quite an experienced bather, and she
could dream of that wonderful experience of being lifted
high above the swells in Donald's strong young arms.

She obediently took her nap, and surrendered herself to
the hands of the maid to have the finishing touches put to
her toilet. It was the soft gray voile that she elected to wear
tonight, and Donald admired her when she emerged from
her room in the dress, looking every inch a lady.

A knock sounded at the door before he had had time to
give Aunt Crete a word of his admiration; but his eyes had
said enough, and she felt a flow of humble pride in her new
self, the self that he had created out of what she had always
considered an unusually plain old woman. With the consciousness of her becoming attire upon her she turned with
mild curiosity to see who had knocked, and, behold, her sister and niece stood before her!

The day had been passed by them in melancholy specula-
tions and the making and abandoning of many plans of
procedure. After careful deliberation they at last concluded
that there was nothing to be done but go down and find out

who these people really were, and if possible allay the ghost of their fears and set themselves free from their dull little room.

"If it should be Aunt Crete and Donald, we'll just settle them up and send them off at once, won't we, Mother?"

"Certainly," said Mrs. Burton with an angry snap to her eyes. "Trust me to settle with your Aunt Crete if it's really her. But I can't think it is. It isn't like Crete one bit to leave her duty. She's got a lot of work to do, and she never leaves her work till it's done. It must be someone else. What if it should be those folks you admire so much? I've been thinking. We had some New York cousins by the name of Ward. It might be one of them, and Donald might have gone to them first, and they've brought him down here. I can't think he's very much, though. But we'll just hope for the best, anyway, till we find out. If it's Aunt Crete, I shall simply talk to her till she is brought to her senses, and make her understand that she's got to go right home. I'll tell her how she's mortifying you, and spoiling your chances of a good match, perhaps——"

"Oh, Ma!" giggled Luella in admiration.

"I'll tell her she must tell Donald she's got to go right home, that the sea air don't agree with her one bit—it goes to her head or something like that, and then we'll make him feel it wouldn't be gallant in him not to take her home. That's easy enough, if 'tis them."

"But Ma, have you thought about your sprained ankle? How 'll they think you got over it so quick? S'posing it shouldn't be Aunt Crete."

"Well, I'll tell her the swelling's gone down, and all of a

sudden something seemed to slip back into place again, and I'm all right."

This was while they were buttoning and hooking each other into their best and most elaborate garments for the peradventure that the people they were to meet might prove to be of patrician class.

They had been somewhat puzzled how to find their possible relatives after they were attired for the advance on the enemy, but consultation with the functionary in the office showed them that, whoever Miss Ward and Donald Grant might be, they surely were at present occupying the apartments on the second floor front.

For one strenuous moment after the elevator had left them before the door of the private parlor they had carefully surveyed each other, fastening a stubborn hook here, putting up a stray rebellious lock there, patting a puff into subordination. Mrs. Burton was arrayed in an elaborate tucked and puffed and belaced lavender muslin whose laborious design had been attained through hours of the long winter evenings past. Luella wore what she considered her most fetching garment, a long, scant, high-waisted robe of fire-red crepe, with nothing to relieve its glare, reflected in staring hues in her already much-burned nose and cheeks. Her hair had been in preparation all the afternoon, and looked as if it was carved in waves and puffs out of black walnut, so closely was it beset with that most noticeable of all invisible devices, an invisible net.

They entered, and stood face to face with the wonderful lady in the gray gown, whose every line and graceful fold spoke of the skill of a foreign tailor. And then, strange to say, it was Aunt Crete who came to herself first.

Perfectly conscious of her comely array, and strong in the strength of her handsome nephew who stood near to protect, she suddenly lost all fear of her fretful sister and bullying niece, and stepped forward with an unconscious grace of welcome that must have been hers all the time,. or it never would have come to the front in this crisis.

"Why, here you are at last, Luella! How nice you look in your red crepe! Why, Carrie, I'm real glad you've got better so you could come down. How is your ankle? And here is Donald. Carrie, can't you see Hannah's looks in him?"

Amazement and embarrassment struggled in the faces of mother and daughter. They looked at Aunt Crete, and they looked at Donald, and then they looked at Aunt Crete again. It couldn't be, it wasn't, yet it was, the voice of Aunt Crete, kind and forgiving, and always thoughtful for everyone, yet with a new something in it. Or was it rather the lack of something? Yes, that was it, the lack of a certain servile something that neither Luella nor her mother could name, yet which made them feel strangely ill at ease with this new-old Aunt Crete.

They looked at each other bewildered, and then back at Aunt Crete again, tracing line by line the familiar features in their new radiance of happiness, and trying to conjure back the worried V in her forehead, and the slinky sag of her old gowns. Was the world turned upside down? What had happened to Aunt Crete?

"Upon my word, Lucretia Ward, is it really you?" exclaimed her sister, making a wild dash into the conversation, determined to right herself and everything else if possible. She felt like a person suddenly upset in a canoe, and she struggled wildly to get her footing once more if there was any solid footing anywhere, with her sister Crete standing there calmly in an imported gown, her hair done up like a fashion plate, and a millionaire's smile on her pleasant face.

But Luella was growing angry. What did Aunt Crete mean by masquerading round in that fashion and making them ashamed before this handsome young man? and was he really their western cousin? Luella felt that a joke was being played upon her, and she always resented jokes—at least, unless she played them herself.

Then Donald came to the front, for he feared for Aunt Crete's poise. She must not lose her calm dignity and get frightened. There was a sharp ring in the other aunt's voice, and the new cousin looked unpromising.

"And is this my aunt Carrie? And my cousin Luella?" He stepped forward, and shook hands pleasantly.

"I am glad to be able to speak with you at last," he said as he dropped Luella's hand, "though it's not the first time I've seen you, nor heard your voice, either, you know."

Luella looked up puzzled, and tried to muster her scattered graces, and respond with her ravishing society air, but somehow the ease and grace of the man before her overpowered her. And was he really her cousin? She tried to think what he could mean by having seen and talked with her before. Surely he must be mistaken, or—perhaps he was referring to the glimpse he had of her when Mr. Grandon bowed the evening before. She tossed her head with a kittenish movement, and arched her poorly pencilled eyebrows.

"Oh, how is that?" she asked, wishing he had not been quite so quick to drop her hand. It would have been more impressive to have had him hold it just a second longer.

"Why, I saw you the morning you left your home, as I was getting out of the train. You were just entering, and you called out of the window to a young lady in a pony cart. You wore a light kind of a yellowish suit, didn't you? Yes, I was very sure it was you."

He was studying her face closely, a curious twinkle in his eyes, which might or might not have been complimentary. Luella could not be sure. The color rose in her cheeks and neck and up to her black-walnut hair till the red dress and the red face looked all of a flame. She suddenly remembered what she had called out to the young lady in the pony cart, and she wondered whether he had heard or noticed.

"And then," went on her handsome persecutor, "I had quite a long talk with you over the telephone, you know——"

"What!" gasped Luella. "Was that you? Why, you must be mistaken, I never telephoned to you; that is, I couldn't get anyone on the phone."

"What's all this about, Luella?" questioned her mother sharply, but Donald interposed.

"Sit down, Aunt Carrie. We are so excited over meeting you at last that we are forgetting to be courteous." He shoved forth a comfortable chair for his aunt, and another for the blushing, overwhelmed Luella, and then he took Aunt Crete's hands lovingly, and gently pushed her backward into the most comfortable rocker in the room. "It's just as easy to sit down, dear Aunt," he said, smiling. "And you know you've had a pretty full day, and must not get tired for tonight's concert at the Casino. Now, Aunt Carrie, tell us about your ankle. How did you come to sprain it so badly, and how did it get well so fast? We were quite alarmed about you. Is it really better? I am afraid you are taxing it too much to have come down this evening. Much as we wanted to see you, we could have waited until it was quite safe for you to use it, rather than have you run any risks."

Then it was the mother's turn to blush, and her thin, somewhat colorless face grew crimson with embarrassment.

"Why, I——" she began; "that is, Luella was working over it, rubbing it with liniment, and all of a sudden she gave it a sort of a little pull, and something seemed to give way with a sharp pain, and then it came all right as good as ever. It feels a little weak, but I think by morning it'll be all right. I think some little bone got out of place, and Luella pulled it back in again. My ankles have always been weak, anyway. I suffer a great deal with them in going about my work at home."

"Why, Carrie," said Aunt Crete, leaning forward with troubled reproach in her face, "you never complained about it."

A dull red rolled over Mrs. Burton's thin features again, and receded, leaving her face pinched and haggard-looking. She felt as if she were seeing visions. This couldn't be her own sister, all dressed up so, and yet speaking in the old sympathetic tone.

"Oh, I never complain, of course. It don't do any good."

The conversation was interrupted by another tap on the door. Donald opened it, and received a large express package. While he was giving some orders to the servant, Mrs. Burton leaned forward, and said in a low tone to her sister:

"For goodness' sake, Lucretia Ward, what does all this mean? How ever did you get decked out like that?"

Then Donald's clear voice broke in upon them as the door

closed once more, and Luella watched him curiously cutting with eager, boyish haste the cords of the express package.

"Aunt Crete, your cloak has come. Now we'll all see if it's becoming."

"Bless the boy," said Aunt Crete, looking up with delighted eyes. "Cloak; what cloak? I'm sure I've got wraps enough now. There's the cloth coat, and the silk one, and that elegant black lace——"

"No, you haven't. I saw right off what you needed when we went out in the auto last night, and I telephoned to that Miss Brower up in the city this morning, and she's fixed it all up. I hope you'll like it."

With that he pulled the cover off the box, and brought to view a long, full evening cloak of pale pearl-colored broadcloth lined with white silk, and a touch about the neck of black velvet and handsome creamy lace.

He held it up at arm's length admiringly.

"It's all right, Aunt Crete. It looks just like you. I knew that woman would understand. Stand up, and let's see how you look in it, and then after dinner we'll take a little spin around the streets to try you in it."

Aunt Crete, blushing like a pretty girl, stood up, and he folded the soft garment about her in all its elegant richness. She stood just in front of the full-length mirror, and could not deny to herself that it was becoming. But she was getting used to seeing herself look well, and was not so much overpowered with the sight as she was with the tender thought of the boy that had got it for her. She forgot Carrie and Luella, and everything but that Donald had gone to great trouble and expense to please her, and she just turned around, and put her two hands, one on each of his cheeks, standing on her tiptoes to reach him, and kissed him.

He bent and returned the kiss laughingly.

"It's a lot of fun to get you things, Aunt Crete," he said; "you always like them so much."

"It is beautiful, beautiful," she said, looking down and smoothing the cloth tenderly as if it had been his cheek. "It's much too beautiful for me. Donald, you will spoil me."

"Yes, I should think so," sniffed Luella, as if offering an apology in some sort for her childish aunt.

"A little spoiling won't hurt you, dear Aunt," said Donald seriously. "I don't believe you've had your share of spoiling yet, and I mean to give it to you if I can. Doesn't she look pretty in it, Cousin Luella? Come now, Aunt Carrie, I suppose it's time to go down to dinner, or we shan't get through in time for the fun. Are you sure your ankle is quite well? Are you able to go to the Casino tonight? I've tickets for us all. Sousa's orchestra is to be there, and the program is an unusually fine one."

Luella was mortified and angry beyond words, but a chance to go to the Casino, in company with Clarence Grandon and his mother, was not to be lightly thrown away, and she crushed down her mortification, contenting herself with darting an angry glance and a hateful curl of her lip at Aunt Crete as they went out the door together. This, however, was altogether lost on that little woman, for she was watching her nephew's face, and wondering how it came that such joy had fallen to her lot.

There was no chance for the mortified mother and daughter to exchange a word as they went down in the elevator or

followed in the wake of their relatives, before whom all porters and office boys and even headwaiters bowed, and
jumped to offer assistance. They were having their wish, to
be sure, entering the dining hall behind the handsome
young man and the elegant, gray-clad, fashionably coiffured
old lady, a part of the train, with the full consciousness of
"belonging," yet in what a way! Both were having ample opportunity for reflection, for they could see at a glance that no
one noticed them, and all attention was for those ahead of
them.

Luella bit her lip angrily, and looked in wonder at Aunt
Crete, who somehow had lost her dumpiness, and walked as
gracefully beside her tall young nephew as if she had been
accustomed to walk in the eyes of the world thus for years.
The true secret of her grace, if Luella had but known it, was
that she was not thinking in the least of herself. Her conscience was at rest now, for the meeting between the cousins
was over, and Luella was to have a good time too. Aunt
Crete was never the least bit selfish. It seemed to her that her
good time was only blooming into yet larger things, after all.

Behind her walked her sister and niece in mortified humiliation. Luella was trying to recall just what she had said
about "country cousins" over the telephone, and exactly
what she had said to the girl in the pony cart the morning
she left home. The memory did not serve to cool her already
heated complexion. It was beginning to dawn upon her that
she had made a mighty mistake in running away from such
a cousin and in such a manner.

All her life, in such a case, Luella had been accustomed to
lay the blame of her disappointments upon someone else,

and vent, as it were, her spite upon that one. Now, in looking about to find such an object of blame her eyes naturally fell upon the one that had borne the greater part of all blame for her. But, try as she would to pour out blame and scorn from her large, bold eyes upon poor Aunt Crete, somehow the blame seemed to slip off from the sweet gray garments, and leave Aunt Crete as serene as ever, with her eyes turned trustingly toward her dear Donald. Luella was brought to the verge of vexation by this, and could scarcely eat any dinner.

The dessert was just being served when the waiter brought Aunt Crete a dainty note from which a faint perfume of violets stole across the table to the knowing nostrils of Luella.

With the happy abandonment of a child Aunt Crete opened it joyously.

"Who in the world can be writing to me?" she said wonderingly. "You'll have to read it for me, Donald; I've left my glasses up in my room."

Luella made haste to reach out her hand for the note, but Donald had it first, as if he had not seen her impatient hand claiming her right to read Aunt Crete's notes.

"It's from Mrs. Grandon, Auntie," he said.

"*Dear Miss Ward,*" he read, "I am sorry that I am feeling too weary to go to the concert this evening as we had planned, and my son makes such a baby of me that he thinks he cannot leave me alone; but I do hope we can have the pleasure of the company of yourself and your nephew on a little auto trip tomorrow afternoon. My brother has a villa a few miles up the shore, and he telephoned us this morning to dine with them tonight. When he heard of your being here, he said by all means to bring you with us. My brother knows of your nephew's friendship with Clarence, and is anxious to meet him, as are the rest of his family. I do hope you will feel able to go with us.

"With sincere regrets that I cannot go with you to the Casino this evening,

HELEN GRANDON."

For the moment Luella forgot everything else in her amazement at this letter. Aunt Crete receiving notes from Mrs. Grandon, from whom she and her mother could scarcely get a frigid bow! Aunt Crete invited on automobile trips and dinners in villas! Donald an intimate friend of Clarence Grandon's! Oh, fool and blind! What had she done! Or what had she undone? She studied the handsome, keen face of her cousin as he bent over the letter, and writhed to think of her own words, "I'm running away from a backwoods cousin"! She could hear it shouted from one end of the great dining hall to the other, and her face blazed redder and redder till she thought it would burst. Her mother turned from her in mortified silence, and wondered why Luella couldn't have had a good complexion.

Studied politeness was the part that Donald had set for himself that evening. He began to see that his victims were sufficiently unhappy. He had no wish to see them writhe under further tortures, though when he looked upon Aunt Crete's happy face, and thought how white it had turned at dread of them, he felt he must let the thorns he had planted in their hearts remain long enough to bring forth a true repentance. But he said nothing further to distress them, and they began to wonder whether, after all, he really had seen through their plan of running away from him.

It was all Aunt Crete's fault. She ought to have arranged it in some way to get them quietly home as soon as she found out what kind of cousin it was that had come to see them. It never occurred to Luella that nothing her poor, abused aunt could have said would have convinced her that her cousin was worthy of her homecoming.

As the concert drew near to its close, Luella and her mother began to prepare for a time of reckoning for Aunt Crete. When she was safely in her room what was to hinder them from going to her alone and having it out? The sister's face hardened, and the niece's eyes glittered as she stonily thought of the scornful sentences she would hurl after her aunt.

Donald looked at her menacing face, and read its thoughts. He resolved to protect Aunt Crete, whatever came; so at the door, when he saw a motion on his Aunt Crete's part to pause, he said gently: "Aunt Crete, I guess we'll have to say good-night now, for you've had a hard day of it, and I want you to be bright and fresh for morning. We want to take an early dip in the ocean. The bathing hours are early tomorrow, I see."

He bowed good-night in his pleasantest manner, and the ladies from the fourth floor reluctantly withdrew to the elevator, but fifteen minutes later surreptitiously tapped at the private door of the room they understood to be Aunt Crete's.

Chapter 7

Luella's Humiliation

The door was opened cautiously by the maid, who was doing Aunt Crete's hair, having just finished a most refreshing facial massage given at Donald's express orders.

Aunt Crete looked round upon her visitors with a rested, rosy countenance, which bloomed out under her fluff of soft, white hair, and quite startled her sister with its freshness and youth. Could it be possible that this was really her sister Crete, or had she made a terrible mistake, and entered the wrong apartment?

But a change came suddenly over the ruddy countenance of Aunt Crete as over the face of a child that in the midst of happy play sees a trouble descending upon it. A look almost of terror came over her, and she caught her breath, and waited to see what was coming.

"Why, Carrie, Luella!" she gasped weakly. "I thought you'd gone to bed. Marie's just doing up my hair for night. She's been giving me a face massage. You ought to try one. It makes you feel young again."

"H'm!" said her affronted sister. "I shouldn't care for one."

Marie looked over Luella and her mother, beginning with

the painfully elaborate arrangement of hair, and going down to the tips of their boots. Luella's face burned with mortification as she read the withering disapproval in the French woman's countenance.

"Let's sit down till she's done," said Luella, dropping promptly on the foot of Aunt Crete's bed and gazing around in frank surprise over the spaciousness of the apartment.

Thereupon the maid ignored them, and went about her work, brushing out and deftly manipulating the wavy white hair, and chattering pleasantly meanwhile, just as if no one else were in the room. Aunt Crete tried to forget what was before her, or, rather, behind her; but her hands trembled a little as they lay in her lap in the folds of the pretty pink and gray challis kimono she wore; and all of a sudden she remembered the unwhitewashed cellar, and the uncooked jam, and the unmade shirtwaists, and the little hot brick house gazing at her reproachfully from the distant home, and she here in this fine array, forgetting it all and being waited upon by a maid—a lazy truant from her duty.

Did the heart of the maid divine the state of things, or was it only her natural instinct that made her turn to protect the pleasant little woman, in whose service she had already been well paid, against the two women that were so evidently of the common walks of life, and were trying to ape those that in the eyes of the maid were their betters? However it was, Marie prolonged her duties a good half hour, and Luella's impatience waxed furious, so that she lost her fear of the maid gradually, and yawned loudly, declaring that Aunt Crete had surely had enough fussing over for one evening.

They held in their more personal remarks until the door finally closed upon Marie, but burst forth so immediately that she heard the opening sentences through the transom, and thought it wise to step to the young gentleman's door and warn him that his elderly relative of whom he seemed so careful was likely to be disturbed beyond a reasonable hour for retiring. Then she discreetly withdrew, having not only added to her generous income by a good bit of silver, but also having followed out the dictates of her heart, which had taken kindly to the gentle woman of the handsome clothes and few pretensions.

"Well, upon my word! I should think you'd be ashamed, Aunt Crete!" burst forth Luella, arising from the bed in a majesty of wrath. "Sitting there, being waited on like a baby, when you ought to be at home this minute earning your living. What do you think of yourself, anyway, living in this kind of luxury when you haven't a cent in the world of your own, and your own sister, who has supported you for years, up in a little dark fourth-floor room? Such selfishness I never saw in all my life. I wouldn't have believed it of you, though we might have suspected it long ago from the foolish things you were always doing. Aunt Crete, have you any idea how much all this costs?"

She waved her hand tragically over the handsome room, including the trunk standing open, and the gleam of silver-gray silk that peeped through the half-open closet door. Aunt Crete fairly cringed under Luella's scornful eyes.

"And you, nothing in the world but a beggar, a *beggar!* That's what you are—a beggar depending upon *us;* and you swelling around as if you owned the earth, and daring to wear silk dresses and real lace collars and expensive jewelry, and even having a maid, and shaming your own relatives, and getting in ahead of us, who have always been good to you, and taking away our friends, and making us appear like two cents! It's just fierce, Aunt Crete! It's—it's *heathenish!*" Luella paused in her anger for a fitting word, and then took the first one that came.

Aunt Crete winced. She was devoted to the Woman's Missionary Society, and it was terrible to be likened to a heathen. She wished Luella had chosen some other word.

"I should think you'd be so ashamed you couldn't hold your head up before your honest relatives," went on the shameless girl. "Taking money from a stranger—that's what he is, a *stranger*—and you whining round and lowering yourself to let him buy you clothes and things, as if you didn't have proper clothes suited to your age and station. He's a young upstart coming along and daring to buy you any— and such clothes! Do you know you're a laughingstock? What would Mrs. Grandon say if she knew whom she was inviting to her automobile rides and dinners? Think of you in your old purple calico washing the dishes at home, and scrubbing the kitchen, and ask yourself what you would say if Mrs. Grandon should come to call on you, and find you that way. You're a hypocrite, Aunt Crete, an awful hypocrite!"

Luella towered over Aunt Crete, and the little old lady looked into her eyes with a horrible fascination, while her great grief and horror poured down her sweet face in tears of anguish that would not be stayed. Her kindly lips were quivering, and her eyes were wide with the tears.

Luella saw that she was making an impression, and she went on more wildly than before, her fury growing with every word, and not realizing how loud her voice was.

"And it isn't enough that you should do all that, but now

you're going to spoil my prospects with Clarence Grandon. You can't keep up this masquerade long, and when they find out what you really are, what will they think of *me?* It'll be all over with me, and it'll be your fault, Aunt Crete, your fault, and you'll never have a happy moment afterwards, thinking of how you spoiled my life."

"Now, Luella," broke in Aunt Crete solemnly through her tears, "you're mistaken about one thing. It won't be my fault there, for it wouldn't have made a bit of difference, poor child. I'm real sorry for you, and I meant to tell you just as soon as we got home, for I couldn't bear to spoil your pleasure while we were here, but that Clarence Grandon belongs to someone else. He isn't for you, Luella, and there must have been some mistake about it. Perhaps he was just being kind to you. For Donald knows him real well, and he says he's engaged to a girl out west, and they're going to be married this fall, and Donald says she's real sweet and——"

But Aunt Crete's quavering voice stopped suddenly in mild affright, for Luella sprang toward her like some mad creature, shaking her finger in her aunt's face, and screaming at the top of her voice:

"It's a lie! I say it's a lie! Aunt Crete, you're a liar; that's what you are with all the rest."

And the high-strung, uncontrolled girl burst into angry sobs.

No one heard the gentle knock that had been twice repeated during the scene, and no one saw the door open until they all suddenly became aware that Donald stood in the room, looking from one face to another in angry surprise.

Donald had not retired at once after bidding Aunt Crete good-night. He found letters and telegrams awaiting his attention, and he had been busy writing a letter of great importance when the maid gave him the hint of Aunt Crete's late callers. Laying down his pen, he stepped quietly across the private parlor that separated his room from his aunt's, and stopped a moment before the door to make sure he heard voices. Then he had knocked, and knocked again, unable to keep from hearing the most of Luella's tirade.

His indignation knew no bounds, and he concluded his time had come to interfere, so he opened the door, and went in.

"What does all this mean?" he asked in a tone that frightened his Aunt Carrie, and made Luella stop her angry sobs in sudden awe.

No one spoke, and Aunt Crete looked a mute appeal through her tears. "What is it, dear Aunt?" he said, stepping over by her side, and placing his arm protectingly round the poor, shrinking little figure, who somehow in her sorrow and helplessness reminded him strongly of his own lost mother. He could not remember at that moment that the other woman, standing hard and cold and angry across the room, was also his mother's sister. She did not look like his mother, nor act like her.

Aunt Crete put her little curled white head in its crisping-pins down on Donald's coat sleeve, and shrank into her pink and gray kimono appealingly as she tried to speak.

"It's just as I told you, Donald, you dear boy," she sobbed out. "I—oughtn't to have come. I knew it, but it wasn't your fault. It was all mine. I ought to have stayed at home, and not dressed up and come off here. I've had a beautiful time, but it wasn't for me, and I oughtn't to have taken it. It's just spoiled Luella's nice time, and she's blaming me, just as I knew she would."

"What does my cousin mean by using that terrible word to you, which I heard as I entered the room?"

Donald's voice was keen and scathing, and his eyes fairly piercing as he asked the question and looked straight at Luella, who answered not a word.

"That wasn't just what she'd have meant, Donald," said Aunt Crete apologetically. "She was most out of her mind with trouble. You see I had to tell her what you told me about that Clarence Grandon being engaged to another girl——"

"Aunt Crete, don't say another word about that!" burst out Luella with flashing eyes and crimson face.

"For mercy's sake, Crete, can't you hold your tongue?" said Luella's mother sharply.

"Go on, Aunt Crete, did my cousin call you a liar for saying that? Yet it was entirely true. If she is not disposed to believe me either, I can call Mr. Grandon in to testify in the matter. He will come if I send for him. But I feel sure, after all, that that will not be necessary. It is probably true, as Aunt Crete says, that you were excited, Luella, and did not mean what you said; and after a good night's sleep you will be prepared to apologize to Aunt Crete, and be sorry enough for worrying her. I am going to ask you to leave Aunt Crete now, and let her rest. She has had a wearying day, and needs to be quiet at once. She is my mother's sister, you know, and I feel as if I must take care of her."

"You seem to forget that I am your mother's sister, too," said Aunt Carrie coldly, as she stood stiff and disapproving beside the door, ready to pass out.

"If I do, Aunt Carrie, forgive me," said Donald courteously. "It is not strange when you remember that you forgot that I was your sister's child, and ran away from me. But
never mind, we will put that aside and try to forget it.
Good-night, Aunt Carrie. Good-night, Cousin Luella. We
will all feel better about it in the morning."

They bowed their diminished heads, and went with
shame and confusion to the fourth floor back; and, when the
door was closed upon them, they burst into angry talk, each
blaming the other, until at last Luella sank in a piteous heap
upon the bed, and gave herself over to helpless tears.

"Luella," said her mother in a businesslike tone, "you
stop that bawling and sit up here and answer me some questions. Did you or did you not go riding with Mr. Clarence
Grandon last winter in his automobile?"

Luella paused in her grief, and nodded assent hopelessly.

"Well, how'd it come about? There's no use sniffing. Tell
me exactly."

"Why, it was a rainy day," sobbed out the girl, "and I met
him on the street in front of the public library the day I'd
been to take back *The Legacy of Earl Crafton,* and that other
book by the same author——"

"Never mind what books; tell me what happened," said
the exasperated mother.

"Well, if you're going to be cross, I shan't tell you anything," was the final reply; and for a moment nothing was
heard in the room but sobs.

However, Luella recovered the thread of her story and
went on to relate how in company with a lot of other girls
she had met Mr. Grandon the day before at the golf links,
where a championship game was being played. She did not

explain the various maneuvers by which she had contrived to be introduced to him, nor that he had not seemed to know her at first when she bowed in front of the library building. She had called out, "It's a fine day for ducks, Mr. Grandon; isn't it good the game was yesterday instead of today?" and he had asked her to ride home with him.

That was her version. Her mother by dint of careful questioning finally arrived at the fact that the girl had more than hinted to be taken home, having loudly announced her lack of rubbers and umbrella, though she seldom wore rubbers, and had on a raincoat and an old hat.

"But how about that big box of chocolates he sent you, Luella? That was a very particular attention to show if he was engaged."

"Oh," pouted Luella, "I don't suppose that meant anything either, for I caught him in a philopena on the way home that day. We said the same words at the same time, something like 'It's going to clear off,' and I told him, when we girls did that, the one that spoke first had to give the other a box of chocolates; so the next day he sent them."

"Luella, I never brought you up to do things like that. I don't think that was very nice."

"Oh, now, Ma, don't you preach. I guess you weren't a saint when you were a girl. Besides, I don't think you're very sympathetic." She mopped her swollen eyes.

"Luella, didn't he ever pay you any more attention after that? I kind of thought you thought he liked you, by the way you talked."

"No, he never even looked at me," sobbed the girl, her grief breaking out afresh. "He didn't even know me the next time we met, but stared straight at me till I bowed, and then he gave me a cold little touch of his hat. And down here he hasn't even recognized me once. I suppose that lady mother of his didn't like my looks."

"Look here, Luella; I wish you'd act sensible. This has been pretty expensive trying to run around after the Grandons. Here's the hotel bills, and all that dress making, and now no telling how Aunt Crete will act after we get home. Like as not she'll think she's got to have a maid, and dress in silks and satins. There's one comfort, probably some of her clothes will fix over for you when she gets off her high horse and comes down to everyday living again. But I wish you'd brace up and forget these Grandons. It's no use trying to get up in the world higher than you belong. There's that nice John Peters who would have been real devoted to you if you'd just let him; and he owns a house of his own already, and has the name of being the best plumber in Midvale."

Luella sighed.

"He's only a plumber, Ma, and his hands are all red and rough."

"Well, what's that?" snapped her practical mother. "He may have his own automobile before long, for all that. Now dry up your eyes, and go to sleep; and in the morning you go down real early, and apologize to your silly Aunt Crete, and make her understand that she's not to disgrace us under any consideration by going bathing while she's here. My land! I expect to see her riding round on one of those saddle ponies on the beach next, or maybe driving that team of goats we saw today, with pink ribbon reins. Come now, Luella, don't you worry. Set out to show your cousin Donald how nice you can be, and maybe some of the silk dresses will come your way. Anyhow, this can't last forever, and John Peters is at home when we get there."

So Luella, soothed in spirit, went to bed, and arose very early the next morning, descending upon poor Aunt Crete while yet the dreams of sailing alone with Donald on a moonlit sea were mingling with her waking thoughts.

Chapter 8

Aunt Crete's Partnership

Luella did her work quietly, firmly, and thoroughly. She vanished before Marie had thought of coming to her morning duties.

At breakfast-time Donald found a sad, cowed little woman waiting for him to go down to the dining room. He tried to cheer her up by telling her how nice a time they were to have in bathing that morning, for the water was sure to be delightful, but Aunt Crete shook her head sadly, and said she guessed she had better not go in bathing anymore. Then she sighed, and looked wistfully out on the blue waves dancing in the sunshine.

"Don't you feel well, Aunt Crete?" asked Donald anxiously.

"Oh, yes, real well," she answered.

"Did it hurt you to go in yesterday, do you think?"

"No, not a mite," she responded promptly.

"Then why in the name of common sense don't you want to go in today? Has Luella been trying to talk some of her nonsense?"

"Well, Luella thinks my figger looks so bad in a bathing suit. She says of course you want to be polite to me, but you don't really know how folks will laugh at me, and make her ashamed of belonging to me."

"Well, I like that!" said Donald. "You just tell Miss Luella we're not running this vacation for her sole benefit. Now, Aunt Crete, you're going in bathing, or else I won't go, and you wouldn't like to deprive me of that pleasure, would you? Well, I thought not. Now come on down to breakfast, and we'll have the best day yet. Don't you let Luella worry you. And, by the way, Aunt Crete, I'm thinking of taking a run up to Cape Cod, and perhaps getting a glimpse of the coast of Maine before I get through. How would you like to go with me?"

"Oh!" gasped Aunt Crete in a daze of delight. "Could I?" Then, mindful of Luella's mocking words the night before: "But I mustn't be an expense to you. I'd just be a burden. You know I haven't a cent of my own in the world, so I couldn't pay my way, and you've done a great deal more than I ought to have let you do."

"Now, Aunt Crete, once for all you must get that idea out of your head. You could never be a burden to me. I want you for a companion. If my mother were here, shouldn't I just love to take her on a journey with me, and spend every cent I had to make her happy? Well, I haven't Mother here; but you are the nearest to Mother I can find, and I somehow feel she'd like me to have you in her place. Will you come? Or is it asking too much to ask you to leave Aunt Carrie and Cousin Luella? They've got each other, and they never really needed you as I do. I've got plenty of money for us to do as we please, and I mean it with all my heart. Will you come and stay with me? I may have to take a flying trip to Europe before the summer's over, and, if I do, it would be dreadfully lonesome to go alone. I think you'd like a trip on the ocean, wouldn't you? and a peep at London, and perhaps Paris and Vienna and old Rome for a few days? And in the fall I'm booked for work in my old university. It's only an assistant professorship yet, but it means a big thing for a young fellow like me, and I want you to come with me and make a cozy little home for me between whiles and a place where I can bring my friends when they get homesick."

He paused and looked down for an answer, and was almost startled by the glory of joy in Aunt Crete's face.

"Oh, Donald, could I do that? Could I be that to you? Do you really think I could be of use enough to you to earn my living?"

He stooped and kissed her forehead reverently to hide the tears that had come unbidden to his eyes. It touched him beyond measure that this sweet life had been so empty of love and so full of drudgery that she should speak thus about so simple a matter. It filled him with indignation against those who had taken the sweetness from her and given her the dregs of life instead.

"Dear Aunt," he said, "you could be of great use to me, and more than earn anything I could do for you many times over, just by being yourself and mothering me; but as for work, there is not to be one stroke done except just what you want to do for amusement. We'll have servants to do all the work, and you shall manage them. I want you for an ornament in my home, and you are going to have a good rest and a continual vacation the rest of your life, if I know anything about it. Now come down to breakfast, so we can go in bathing early, and don't you worry another wrinkle about Luella. You don't belong to her anymore. We'll send her a parasol from New York and a party gown from Paris, and she won't bother her pompadour anymore about you, you may be sure."

In a maze of delight Aunt Crete went down to breakfast, and dawned upon the astonished vision of her sister and niece in all the beauty of her dainty white morning costume. They were fairly startled at the vision she was in white, with her pretty white hair to match it. Luella gasped and held her disapproving breath, but Aunt Crete was too absorbed in the vision of joy that had opened before her to know or care what they thought of her in a white dress.

No girl in the new joy of her first love was ever in a sweeter dream of bliss than was Aunt Crete as she beamed through her breakfast. Luella's looks of scorn and Luella's mother's sour visage had no effect upon her whatever. She smiled happily, and ate her breakfast in peace, for had she not been set free forever from the things that had made her life a burden heretofore, and shown into a large place of new joys where her heart might find rest?

After breakfast Donald made them all walk down the boardwalk to the various shops filled with curios, where he bought everything that Luella looked at, and lavished several gifts also upon her mother, including a small Oriental rug that she admired. They returned to the hotel in a good humor, and Luella began to have visions of luxurious days to come. She felt sure she could keep Aunt Crete down about where she wanted her, and her eyes gloated over the beautiful white dress that she hoped to claim for her own when they all went home and she had convinced Aunt Crete how unsuitable white was for old ladies.

She was quite astonished, after her morning talk with her aunt, to hear Donald say as he looked at his watch, "Come, Aunt Crete, it's time for our bath," and to see Aunt Crete walk smiling off toward the bathhouses, utterly regardless of her wrathful warning glances. It was rather disconcerting to have Aunt Crete become unmanageable right at the beginning this way. But in view of the fact that her hands were filled with pretty trifles bought by her cousin she did not feel like making any protest beyond threatening glances, which the dear soul whose mind was in Europe, and whose heart was in a cozy little home all her own and Donald's, did not see at all.

Aunt Crete was happy. She felt it in every nerve of her body as she stepped into the crisp waves and bounded out to meet them with the elasticity of a girl.

Luella, following a moment later in her flashy bathing suit of scarlet and white, watched her aunt in amazement, and somehow felt that Aunt Crete was drifting away from her, separated by something more than a few yards of blue salt water.

Donald kept up a continual flow of bright conversation during the noon meal, and managed to engage Luella and her mother on the long piazza in looking through the marine glass at a great ship that went lazily floating by, while Aunt Crete was getting ready to go on the ride; and before Luella and her mother were quite aware of what was happening they stood on the piazza watching Aunt Crete in her handsome black crepe de chine, which even boasted a modest train, and her black lace wrap and bonnet, being handed into the Grandon motorcar, while Donald carried her long new gray cloak on his arm. The gray car moved smoothly away out of sight, and Luella and her mother were left staring at the sea with their own bitter reflections.

The automobile party did not return until late that night, for the moon was full and the roads were fine, and Donald saw to it that Aunt Crete was guarded against any intrusion.

It was at breakfast next morning that Donald told them, and Aunt Crete sat listening with the rapt smile that a slave might have worn as he listened to the reading of the proclamation of emancipation.

"Aunt Carrie," he began as pleasantly as if he were about to propose that they all go rowing, "Aunt Crete and I have decided to set up a permanent partnership. She has consented to come and mother me. I have accepted a position in my old university, and I am very tired of boarding. I think we shall have a cozy, pleasant home; and we'll be glad to have you and Luella come and visit us sometimes after we get settled and have some good servants so that Aunt Crete will have plenty of time to take you around and show you the sights. In the meantime, it is very likely that I may have to take a brief trip abroad for the university. If so, I shall probably start in about a week, and before that I want to get a glimpse of the New England coast. I have decided to take Aunt Crete, and run away from you today. We leave on the noon train; so there is time for a little frolic yet. Suppose we go down to the boardwalk, and eat an ice-cream cone. I saw some delicious ones last night that made my mouth water, and we haven't had that experience yet. We'll get some rolling chairs so that Aunt Crete won't be too tired for her journey. Come, Aunt Crete, you won't need to go upstairs again, shall you? I told Marie about the packing. It won't be necessary for you to go back until it's time for you to change to your traveling garb."

In a daze of anger and humiliation Luella and her mother climbed into their double rolling chair, and ate their ice cream cones sullenly, propelled by a large boy; but Aunt Crete had a chair to herself, and was attended by Donald, who kept up a constant stream of delightfully funny conversation about the people and things they passed that made Aunt Crete laugh until the tears came into her happy eyes.

There was no opportunity for Luella and her mother to talk to Aunt Crete alone, even after they returned to the hotel, for Donald kept himself in evidence everywhere, until at last Luella made bold to declare that she didn't see why Donald thought he had a right to come and take Aunt Crete away from them, when they had always taken care of her; and her mother added in an injured tone:

"Yes, you don't seem to realize what a burden it's been all these years, having to support Crete, and her so childish and unreasonable in a great many ways, and not having any idea of the value of money. I've spent a good deal on Crete, take it all in all; and now, when Luella's going out, and has to have clothes and company, it's rather hard to have her leave us in the lurch this way, and me with all the work to do."

"That being the case, Aunt Carrie," said Donald pleasantly, "I should suppose you'd be very glad to have me relieve you of the burden of Aunt Crete's support, for it will be nothing but a pleasure to me to care for her the rest of her life. As for what you have spent for her, just run it over in your mind, and I shall be quite glad to reimburse you. Aunt Crete is really too frail and sweet to have to work any longer. I should think my cousin was almost old enough to be a help to you now, and she looks perfectly strong and able to work."

Luella flashed a vindictive glance at her cousin, and turned haughtily toward the window; then the porter came for the trunks, and the travelers said a hasty good-bye, and flitted.

As Donald shook hands with Luella in parting, he looked merrily into her angry eyes, and said:

"I do hope, Luella, that it hasn't been too much of a trial to have your 'backwoods cousin' spend a few days here. You'll find a box of bonbons up in your room, if the porter did his duty, which may sweeten your bitter thoughts of me; and we hope you'll have a delightful time the remainder of your stay here. Goodbye."

* * *

About three months after Donald had returned from Europe and settled to his western university life Aunt Crete received a letter from her sister. It was brief and to the point, and Aunt Crete could read between the lines. It read:

> *Dear Crete*—Aren't you about sick of that nonsense, and ready to come home? Luella has decided that she can't do better than take John Peters. He has promised to buy an auto next year, if the plumbing business keeps up. I think at least you might come home and help get her things ready, for there's a great deal of sewing to do, and you know I can't afford to hire it; and Luella's out so much, now she's engaged. Do come soon.
> Your sister, CARRIE.

Aunt Crete looked sober, but Donald, looking over her shoulder, read, and then went to his desk for a moment.

Coming back, he dropped a check for five hundred dollars into his aunt's lap.

"Send her that from me, Aunt Crete, and another from yourself, if you like, and let her hire the sewing done. They don't want you, and I do."

Aunt Crete had her own bank account now, thanks to her thoughtful nephew, and she smiled back a delighted, "I will," and went off to write the letter, for Aunt Crete was at last emancipated.